NOT OVER YOU

SAMANTHA WAYLAND

ALSO BY SAMANTHA WAYLAND

Not Over You

Copyright © 2023 Samantha Wayland

Published by Loch Awe Press

P.O. Box 5481

Wayland, MA 01778

ISBN 978-1-940839-34-9 (eBook)

ISBN 978-1-940839-35-6 (paperback)

Edited by PNWSandy Edits at KRS Author Services

Proofread by Lori Parks

Cover Art by Ben Ellis, Tall Story Design

Content/Sensitivity Edit by Renita McKinney

For Aly, a generous source of sanity, encouragement, and Girl Scout cookies.

1

Hunter Michaelson had a lot on his mind.

He wasn't a guy who traditionally spent a great deal of time ruminating on life. He just *lived* it. And that had clearly worked out for him since he had a pretty great life—deep thoughts or no deep thoughts, he wasn't complaining. Hell, he got paid ridiculous amounts of money to play hockey, the greatest sport in the world, in an awesome city.

But as much as he loved hockey—and he hella loved hockey— one of the best parts of his job was the off-season. He'd come home to Moncton for a month over the summer and spend time with his parents and friends, including Callum Morrison. He was damn lucky to have had Callum as a mentor when he had been a dumb rookie, and felt even luckier now, six years later, to count Callum as a friend. He understood the shit Hunter dealt with—as an athlete and as someone in the public eye—in a way very few people could.

Better even than Hunter had realized until the conversation they'd had over a couple of beers last summer. It hadn't seemed momentous at the time, but it had burrowed under Hunter's skin, laying the groundwork for something Hunter refused to think of as an existential crisis but maybe looked like one if he squinted.

So, here he was, four months later, having dragged his ass back up to Moncton for the four-day Christmas break. Normally, it wasn't enough time to make a trip home worth it, but he needed to talk to Callum. In person. Even if it meant connecting through Toronto and quality time spent with ten thousand short-tempered holiday travelers.

Now it was Christmas Eve and the moment of truth had arrived.

Callum had generously invited Hunter over to his weird but super-cool house on the top floor of what appeared from the outside to be a shitty warehouse. Inside was a warm and welcoming family home, with stockings hung from the dark wood mantle above a cheerful fire and giant red poinsettias scattered throughout the house.

Hunter was parked on a stool on the far side of the island that formed a barrier between the kitchen and the open living room and dining room spaces. The reflection of the enormous Christmas tree behind him added sparkles to the doors of the double ovens in which Callum was roasting a huge rib roast *and* baking a pie.

By some stroke of luck, they had the house to themselves, though Hunter knew from experience that this was unlikely to last.

Hunter watched in amazement as Callum moved between the stove, the ovens, and the countertops, doing ten things at once. It was hard to reconcile this Callum with the one Hunter had played with in Denver. That man had been quiet and cynical, even a touch bitter. He'd always been kind to Hunter and the other guys on the team, but he hadn't been happy. He certainly hadn't been a man who would smile cheerfully while sticking his face in the steam rising off a pot on the stove and gush about how his cherry red minivan had been perfectly detailed the week before.

This Callum was content. Settled. And Hunter couldn't be happier for him.

The trick was, Hunter wanted to be happier for himself, too.

Callum plunked a mug of coffee onto the butcher block counter in front of Hunter. "How are things in Pittsburgh?"

Hunter curled his hands around the warm ceramic, rubbing the smooth glaze with his thumb while Callum studied him from across the counter.

"The guys are great, and the season is going well." Hunter cringed, because why the fuck was he using his media voice?

Callum arched an eyebrow, apparently wondering the same thing.

Hunter sighed. "Sorry. I mean it, though. Pittsburgh is great. Way cooler than I thought it would be."

"Good. I remember you were worried when you got traded." Callum had been the first to reassure Hunter at the time and was kind enough not to say *I told you so* now. "So, what's going on?"

Hunter wet his lips, trying to figure out what he wanted to say while Callum pulled a mountain of produce out of the fridge. Hunter had come here to talk but now he felt stuck, his palms damp and his heartbeat too fast. He didn't get this anxious before playoff games, for Christ's sake.

Callum stacked the vegetables on the island across from Hunter and gave him a long look.

"I bought a house," Hunter announced, because he had to start somewhere. "I didn't want to live in a high-rise anymore and I found this great place at the end of a cul-de-sac that's up against the park. Right downtown, but you'd never know it. I've been living in a construction zone all season, but I'm hoping my contractor will finish my bedroom next week, so I have a place to hide while he wraps up everything else."

Hunter stopped his babbling with a long sip of his coffee.

Callum nodded and kept chopping a carrot into tiny cubes, no doubt keeping busy to give Hunter space.

Some people had been surprised when Callum suddenly became the enthusiastic father of three. Hunter was sure none of those people had ever met Callum. He'd had this dad thing down years ago.

Hunter reminded himself that he'd always trusted Callum. That he could be honest with him and expect the same in return.

"What did you mean when you said you had a lot of regrets?"

Callum put down the knife and gave Hunter his full attention. "Come again?"

"I just—" Hunter swallowed, his throat dry. "This summer, I asked if you would change anything about your career and you said you had a lot of regrets about how you let hockey be your excuse for not doing things or being yourself, and I guess I've been thinking about that."

Nonstop. For four months.

Callum nodded and took a moment before he answered. Usually Hunter appreciated Callum's thoughtfulness, but his steady gaze on Hunter's face was making him sweaty.

"You don't have to talk about it," Hunter added, realizing too late that bombing in on a guy and asking him to spill his regrets was probably rude. It was Hunter's problem if he didn't trust anyone else as much, let alone believe they would understand.

"I don't mind talking about it," Callum said. "But it would help if I had a better idea of where you're coming from." His smile was wry. "I have quite a few regrets and I don't want to bore you with the wrong ones."

Hunter wanted to say Callum could talk about all of them, as much as he wanted, but Hunter was also aware of the time, the date, and that they were increasingly likely to lose this privacy every minute he dragged this out.

"I...uh...I've been thinking about what you said. Just a little"—he cringed internally at the whopping lie—"and I think I've been doing some of those things, too."

"Things you regret?" Callum asked, expression concerned.

"No—well, yes. But no."

Callum arched that eyebrow again.

"I'm not going out and doing dumb stuff or anything like that. Don't worry. I'm just...not dating anymore."

Callum nodded like he was following when Hunter knew he wasn't making any fucking sense.

He tried to explain. "Because I was dating the wrong...uh, people.

And I stopped because I thought about what you said and I didn't want to regret it, in the long run."

"That sounds smart," Callum ventured, kind enough to not make it sound like a question.

Hunter let out a nervous laugh. "Yeah, I think so, too. And Pittsburgh is different. My neighborhood is near UPitt and Carnegie Mellon, so there are a lot of younger people. You know, doing their thing."

"Doing their thing," Callum repeated.

"Yeah. Just...being themselves. Being"—*Fucking say it, Hunter* —"open, if you know what I mean."

"Ah," Callum said just as a timer went off. He turned to the oven, trying to hide a smile while he poked at the roast.

Hunter took courage from that. "Anyway, what you said really got me thinking about how much of my life has been dictated by hockey. And I guess...I guess I'm kind of worried about that. Because I love hockey. It's always been the dream. And here I am and I'm so lucky, and I know that, and I love my team and the guys, and I have some really good friends in that group, and I don't want to lose that. But I don't want regrets, either."

By the end, it was all just pouring out of Hunter—his voice too high, the words too fast.

Callum closed the oven, wiped his hands on his apron, and came around the island. Hunter wondered if he was about to get a pity hug, but Callum pulled out a stool and sat facing him, close enough that their knees touched. He gave Hunter his undivided attention, his concern and affection obvious, and Hunter felt the weirdest urge to cry and beg for that hug, pitiful or not.

Fuck. This was supposed to be the easy part. In the list of ways to change his course that Hunter had come up with, this—talking to Callum—was supposed to be one of the simple things. His conversation with Callum had forced him to face the need for change, so telling Callum about it should be easy, right?

Apparently not. Maybe there would be no easy parts. Maybe

Hunter would continually feel like the rug had been yanked out from under him and he was midair with no idea how to land on his feet.

THERE WAS little that truly frightened Zach Bloom, but public speaking was one of them, and the prospect of standing up in front of Dr. Sorenson's freshman Intro to Lit class was easily in the top three on his List of Terrifying Things.

"You're going to do brilliantly," Barnaby, his friend—and mentor, of sorts—said with the enthusiastic relish only the delusional could achieve.

Zach huffed. "Even *you* don't believe that."

Barnaby grinned, like Zach's terror was amusing. "I do. I know you're a bit nervous, but you'll be fine once you're in the thick of it."

Barnaby made it sound so easy. Maybe it was the English accent, which to Zach's ears made everything sound better than it was.

Or maybe that was the lingering traces of Zach's crush talking. Fortunately, Zach had recovered from the worst of his infatuation, helped along by Barnaby being completely in love with his boyfriend and oblivious to any other man on earth.

It would have been nauseating if it weren't so fucking cute.

Zach pictured the massive lecture hall and the stage he'd be expected to stand on, and his stomach lurched again.

Maybe Barnaby would take Zach's problem more seriously if Zach upchucked on his shoes.

Swallowing against the bile crawling up his throat, Zach threw away the dregs of his coffee and followed Barnaby out the door of the Dipsy Doodle Dangle Café. The fresh cold air felt good on Zach's cheeks, helping to clear his head and settle his stomach.

"I just don't like to be the center of attention," Zach explained.

"I know," Barnaby said, bumping his shoulder companionably against Zach's as they walked toward the city center and the river. "Though I still don't understand how being a goalie for the university's hockey team works with that."

Zach shrugged. "I don't know. It's not the same. It's just a school team, and not a particularly good one at that."

Barnaby hummed, and Zach hoped he hadn't opened the door for another discussion about playing professional hockey. Zach didn't want that, never had, and no amount of compliments or suggestions or even outright contract offers was going to change that.

Barnaby's boyfriend, Travis, was a scout for the Moncton Ice Cats and had approached Zach about the possibility of playing for them after watching one of his games. Zach had been deeply flattered but hadn't hesitated to turn down the offer.

Zach enjoyed playing hockey, but his dreams lay elsewhere. He was determined to one day be able to support himself with his writing while traveling the world.

Zach liked to move around, physically and geographically, but also loved school. He was content to be one of the older undergraduates on campus after taking time off to travel whenever he'd saved up sufficient funds. His parents had despaired when he'd been younger that he'd never excel in academia, but those years off, and just getting older, had gone a long way toward helping him settle into school. He was lucky the university had needed his skills in goal enough to let him back on the team after a year off, but he would have given up hockey before he'd missed the opportunity to travel through Vietnam. Or Japan. Or Ethiopia.

Now he had a good balance going. He burned off any excess energy through hockey or a run and could spend hours poring over books and at his laptop—writing for school or for pleasure and working as a copy editor. And on the days the jitters didn't dissipate through his usual outlets, Zach took advantage of the fact that most professors understood the benefits of allowing a student to stand in the back of the room for their lecture.

It was standing in the *front* of the room that freaked Zach out.

"I can't believe he's asking me to do this," Zach said, not for the first time. "You were his TA all last year. You should do it."

"You know I don't have a choice. Can you imagine if I told my dissertation advisor to fuck off and find a different TA so I can work for Sorenson again? I need him to like me," Barnaby reminded him.

Zach understood that, and that it was an honor to be asked to step in.

Zach *was* honored. Really.

It just sucked.

"Anyway, once you look through all my notes and materials, you'll see the TA piece is very simple," Barnaby continued, still delusional.

"But I'm an undergrad. I'm—"

"Come on, Zach. You're more of an adult than half my fellow doctoral candidates. You know this stuff upside-down and front-to-back. And we both know having a TA job on your CV will make you more attractive to graduate programs."

Zach sighed. "I know. And I can't thank you enough."

Barnaby laughed. "You could try to sound like you mean it."

"I do mean it. I know why this is a good idea. It's just hard to get excited about the prospect of vomiting in front of a hundred freshmen."

"You won't vomit. The worst that will happen is you'll be a little wooden the first couple of times you have to do the announcements. After that, I'm sure you'll be fine," Barnaby said with wildly misplaced optimism. "Dr. Sorenson only punts to his TAs for a couple of classes each semester and for leading the study groups, which, as you know, are only a dozen students each. I seem to recall you practically led your group as a student last year, and you knew the material as well as I did."

Zach shrugged. "Sorry? I do get excited about this stuff."

"No one should apologize for liking school, let alone being good at it."

Barnaby was right, of course. And while writing was Zach's passion, school was his top priority for now, even above hockey. And definitely above any kind of romantic relationship. He'd learned that lesson when his plan of putting off school to follow his boyfriend to a new city, whatever city, had proven to be a fantasy.

Thank god. No matter how much it had hurt, he had no regrets and only good things to look forward to, including, hopefully, one of the graduate programs to which he'd recently applied.

After a lifetime of Moncton being his home base, he was eager to try living in New York, Boston, or Pittsburgh—depending on which program he ended up attending.

There was nothing holding him here other than a few friends he could always come back to visit. Hell, even his parents had moved away last year, so it wasn't like he was leaving the nest. The nest had relocated to the goddamn Cayman Islands without him.

Shaking his head at himself—and his parents—Zach followed Barnaby across the street toward the warehouse at the end of the road that loomed over the river beyond. He eyed the massive ugly building.

"You sure this is where we're going?"

Barnaby laughed. "I do think I know how to find my way home."

Zach wasn't convinced, since he was certain Barnaby and Travis lived in a converted Victorian not too far on the other side of the downtown area. Before that, though, he'd lived with—

Zach's brain came to a screeching halt, the proverbial needle scratching across vinyl. He stumbled to a halt. "Wait. Are we...are you taking me to *Callum Morrison's* house?"

Barnaby looked back over his shoulder at Zach standing in the middle of the street and frowned. "Yes. Of course. I told you I stored all my coursework at home. Callum and Rupert have been kind enough to let me leave a handful of boxes with them, since Travis and I don't have a lot of space in our apartment."

"But...*Callum Morrison*," Zach said stupidly.

"*Yeeess*." Barnaby dragged the word out like Zach was being weird instead of having a perfectly understandable reaction to learning he was about to enter the home of his fucking hero. "You are aware he's married to my cousin, aren't you? I'm sure we've discussed this. I seem to recall you squealing like a fanboy over lattes in the student union, or am I mistaken?"

"Shut up," Zach muttered, cheeks burning.

"Oh god, is this one of those *goalie things*?" Barnaby asked, complete with air quotes.

"No," Zach said defensively. Then, "Shit. Okay, yes. But...he's *Callum Morrison*."

"Callum Smythe-Morrison, actually. Do try to remember that as I introduce you and you're coming in your pants."

Zach gasped. "I would never!"

"Oh good. We apparently *do* have a limit to this goalie fanboy thing. Now, are you ready to go get the materials for your first outing as a teacher to hundreds?"

Zach could feel the color draining from his face. "That was just mean."

"It worked, didn't it?" Barnaby resumed walking.

Zach followed, albeit reluctantly. "I don't know what to say."

"I'd start with *hello*. Maybe a *nice to meet you*. Honestly, Zach, Callum is—"

"A god?" Zach asked, because how did Barnaby not know?

Barnaby snorted. "I was going to say a giant dork. If you don't believe me, ask him about his minivan. He loves that thing almost as much as he does Rupert and the children."

Zach frowned, following Barnaby through a door in the side of the warehouse and into a massive empty storage space. Or what should have been a storage space, but appeared to be a garage, a basketball court, and a gym at the moment.

And it didn't get any less weird from there. The elevator could have fit his entire team—with their gear on—and rattled worse than the hayride Zach had taken his friends on for his tenth birthday, during which a wheel had come clean off the damn wagon.

Elevator rides were not anywhere on Zach's List of Terrifying Things, which was good or this ride might have stroked him out.

Once they'd come to a jarring halt, Barnaby pried opened the doors to reveal an incongruously elegant hallway. Zach admired the wainscoting and deep carpets and wondered if he'd stepped through the wardrobe and into Narnia.

Barnaby pulled a key from his pocket and opened the door to apartment 4B.

"I just have to dig through the storage closet," Barnaby explained. "So I'll leave you here with Callum." Barnaby stepped into a large, high-ceilinged industrial space into which someone had shoehorned the entire contents of a European manor house. "Oh, he has a guest."

Zach tugged off his hat and marshalled his meager social skills. He was not going to make an ass of himself. He was not going to make an ass of himself. He was—

Callum Smythe-Morrison, Zach's fucking *hero*, rose to his feet with a warm smile on his face.

Zach smiled back, awestruck but still prepared to apologize for interrupting, when Callum's guest turned to face them.

Then the whole world stopped.

2

A heavy silence seemed to fill every inch of the huge apartment while Hunter and Zach stared at each other. Hunter's legs felt numb as he stood, his grip on the counter the only reason he didn't sway on his feet.

Had he somehow conjured the very embodiment of his regrets? The ones he'd told himself didn't exist, but somehow still had a name and a face.

For almost six years, he'd braced himself for this moment every time he came back to Moncton, hoping for it and dreading it in turns. He'd thought of what to say. How to act.

But nothing could have prepared him for the devastating effect of seeing Zachary Bloom in person again.

Zach stood frozen, pale except for two bright red spots high on his cheekbones. Hunter vividly recalled pressing his own cheeks to those spots to feel their heat. How the texture of the skin along Zach's jaw had changed from smooth to stubble-rough toward the end of high school.

Toward the end of them.

Hunter swallowed, his eyes running over Zach. He'd already been a couple inches over six feet by the time they were halfway through high school, but he wasn't a beanpole anymore. His shoulders were wider, and he carried more muscle all over, filled out in ways that made his snug, worn jeans seem vaguely obscene.

Zach's thick brown hair, in total disarray from his poor attempt to finger-comb it after he'd tugged off his hat, was exactly how Hunter remembered it best. If he closed his eyes, Hunter swore he could still feel the silky curls against his face and neck. His shoulders. His thighs.

Hunter dared to meet Zach's big, brown eyes, and it still felt like Zach looked right through all the bullshit and directly into his soul.

That didn't use to hurt.

Suddenly, Zach's eyes darted to Hunter's left. Probably because the man Zach had worshipped all through childhood was standing there.

Bumping into Hunter likely paled in comparison to that.

"Callum," Hunter said, his voice jarring after the protracted silence. "Do you know Zach?"

The man who had led Zach into the apartment cocked his head. Belatedly, Hunter noticed he was fucking gorgeous and vaguely familiar. Was this Zach's boyfriend? He certainly seemed concerned about Zach, based on the inquisitive looks and the gentle touch to Zach's arm.

Hunter forced himself to look away from the stupidly attractive men across the room only to find Callum watching him, eyebrows up, curiosity written all over his face. Hunter narrowed his eyes and glared back.

Callum took the hint and turned back to the new arrivals. "Right. Hello!" He thrust his hand toward Zach. "Welcome."

"Thank you. I mean, hi. Hello." Zach's eyes were the size of saucers. "I'm Zach. My name is Zach. Bloom."

Apparently, Zach was still shy. And Hunter still found it painfully charming.

Callum, no lie, gasped like he'd gotten an early Christmas present. "I know you! You're the goalie for Moncton University, right?"

His handshake rocked Zach's arm all the way up to his shoulder. "I've seen you in net. You're *so* good."

Zach's bright flush of embarrassment spread from his cheeks all the way to his hairline, even as he practically glowed with happiness. "Oh, wow. Thank you so much. Coming from you that's...yeah. *Wow.*"

"Zach's always been a big fan of yours, Callum," Hunter said, leaning into years of media training to keep his voice steady. It also made him sound detached and like a douchebag giving lip service. He dropped the bullshit. "He watched all your games. He even had your poster—"

The noise Zach made bore a strong resemblance to Hunter's cat ejecting a hairball.

Ten seconds too late, Hunter realized why Callum's poster had been pinned to the ceiling above Zach's bed. He stifled a totally inappropriate guffaw and released an unattractive snort instead.

So much for media training.

The stranger who'd brought Zach stepped forward and held out his hand. "I'm Barnaby, Zach's friend from school and Rupert's cousin."

Which explained how Barnaby came to have a key to this apartment and where Hunter might have seen him before—the wedding.

"Hunter Michaelson," he said, clasping Barnaby's hand. "I played with Callum in Denver." When Barnaby looked pointedly between Zach and Hunter, Hunter added, "And with Zach in high school."

"Ah," Barnaby and Callum said in unison before Callum pulled Barnaby in for a hug and kissed the top of his head in a total dad move. Barnaby hugged Callum back, a pleased smile curving his lips.

The dude really was unfairly attractive.

"So, what are you boys doing here?" Callum asked once he'd released Barnaby. "Dinner isn't for at least another hour."

Before Barnaby could answer, the door to the apartment burst open and Callum's family, loaded down with shopping bags, poured in. They were led by Oliver, who announced their arrival for those who may have missed the door bouncing off the wall.

"We're here!" the eight-year-old bellowed.

Callum's face lit up and he reached for Rupert, who was arguing with a large Russian man Hunter recognized as Alexei Belov, the long-time starting goalie for the Moncton Ice Cats. Rupert paused to drop his bags on the counter, kiss Callum's cheek, and shift their two-year-old daughter, Eleanor, onto Callum's hip.

Hunter felt a rush of envy, and not just because Zach stared at Callum like he'd hung the moon. He wondered if Zach still had that poster.

Rupert went to Barnaby next and gave him a brief, awkward hug that seemed to please them both.

Then Rupert smiled at Zach. "Hello, I'm Rupert."

Before Zach could respond, Alexei finished dropping his bags by the door and looked over, his eyes widening.

"*Zachary Bloom!*" Rupert, Zach, Barnaby, and Hunter all jumped when Alexei's booming voice shook the rafters. The huge man bore down on Zach. "What are you doing here?"

Zach grinned, his face transformed. "Alexei!"

Their hug looked like it might hurt. Hunter stamped down the irrational urge to drag Zach away from the massive man with his paws all over him.

"I see you've met," Rupert observed dryly from where he'd been forced aside.

"Yes, yes," Alexei said. "This is Zachary Bloom. He's a wonderful goalie."

"Ah, yes," Rupert said as he shook Zach's hand. "I've heard good things. I believe Travis tried to recruit you to back up Alexei here, but we lost out to graduate school?"

Zach's blush returned with a vengeance, which Hunter guessed was at least twenty percent due to Zach's accent kink. Though Hunter didn't miss that the Ice Cats wanted Zach to go pro.

It was almost reassuring that *this* hadn't changed—Zach hadn't wanted to become a professional hockey player six years ago, either. And maybe Hunter understood why a little better now.

A flurry of introductions followed, including Callum and Rupert's teenage son, Christian, and Alexei's fiancé, Mike. Somehow, in the shuffle of people, purchases, food, and drinks, Hunter ended up holding his coffee mug and watching the chaos from the living room, not far from the front door. He considered slipping out and catching up with Callum later, but he didn't want to leave.

He wanted to finish his conversation with Callum.

He wanted to watch Zach in the kitchen with Alexei, where he was being pressed into service. The alarm on Zach's face as Alexei held out an apron was priceless. Zach held up his hands and shook his head, which Alexei took as an opportunity to put the apron over Zach's head, before spinning him around to tie it.

Hunter didn't register the gentle knock behind him until the door almost hit him.

"Oh! Sorry!" a man said as he slipped into the apartment. He was handsome, blond, and, Hunter would bet money, another hockey player.

Hockey butt didn't lie.

"No worries. I'm standing in the wrong spot," Hunter said as he stepped further into the living room.

He might as well have been talking to himself because the newest arrival only had eyes for Barnaby. He made a beeline to the beautiful man, caught him around the waist, and dipped him back to plant a kiss on his lips.

Barnaby smiled and kissed him in return, barely pausing in his discussion with Rupert.

Hunter ached at the sweet display while also experiencing a keen relief he had no business feeling. So what if Barnaby wasn't Zach's boyfriend? Hunter had no claim on Zach. Hell, Zach would probably like nothing better than to kick him in the nuts and forget he ever existed.

A gentle hand on Hunter's shoulder startled him so badly his coffee sloshed over the rim of his mug and onto his boot.

Callum grimaced. "Sorry. You doing okay?"

Hunter sighed. "Yeah."

Callum studied Hunter's face. "You sure?"

"I am. Really." Hunter looked at Zach and wondered if it was true.

"You still want to talk about regret?" Callum never did miss much.

Hunter snorted. "You know, when I got here, it was an abstract concept I'd been thinking about."

"And now?"

"It's a lot more concrete."

Callum gripped Hunter's shoulder in his big, warm hand. "Sadly, you can't always fix the past."

"I know. But sometimes it's hard not to wonder how things might have been different, even if it's probably better they turned out the way they did." He glanced at Callum but couldn't help but look back at Zach again. "And sometimes you have to admit that, if you don't make some changes, you're going to regret what happens next, you know?"

"I do know," Callum said quietly. "Only too well."

Hunter nodded. "That's what you got me thinking about, I guess."

"Should I apologize?"

"No. In fact, I should thank you." And it was true. Hunter *was* grateful Callum had inadvertently shoved Hunter off the path he had been traveling.

Callum threw an arm over Hunter's shoulders and gave him a side hug. "It's nice to think you younger guys aren't going to make a huge fucking hash of things like I did."

Hunter chuckled. He hadn't avoided making a huge fucking hash of it yet, but he appreciated Callum's optimism. "Yeah, well, we'll see."

"So, what's the first step?" Callum asked.

Zach laughed at something Alexei said, and Hunter's heart ached at the familiar sound. "I have no idea."

Callum pursed his lips thoughtfully. "Well, maybe I do. How about you stay for dinner?"

Hunter's parents were at a cocktail thing with neighbors and Hunter would rather poke his own eye out than attend that, so he nodded. "That would be great. Thank you. Though I don't know how that's going to help."

Callum gave his shoulders a last squeeze, whapped his ass hard enough to sting, then sauntered into the kitchen. "Hey, Zach! You're staying for dinner, right?"

ZACH BLINKED AT CALLUM SMYTHE-MORRISON. *The* Callum Smythe-Morrison. "Uh…"

"I mean, I know it's Christmas Eve, so if you need to get going—"

"I'm Jewish."

Callum nodded like that was a helpful answer and Zach wasn't Captain Awkward. "Cool. So…dinner?"

Zach gave himself a mental kick in the ass. "I mean to say, I have no plans because my family doesn't celebrate this holiday, but I'd be honored to help celebrate it with yours."

"Great!" Callum said with a big smile.

Alexei whacked Zach on the back enthusiastically. "Wonderful, you can help me carve the roast!"

Zach grinned. Dinner with this family sounded a hell of a lot better than eating whatever leftovers he had alone. It was bound to be fun hanging out with Alexei somewhere other than at the rink after a game. Alexei had come to watch him play a few times, which is how they'd become friends, of a sort. Not come-to-the-house-for-major-holidays friends, but it didn't seem too weird that Zach was here, wearing an apron that proudly proclaimed *Give blood! Play hockey!*

The whole thing would have been perfect were it not for the quiet, brooding presence in the corner by the door. Zach wished he could ignore Hunter. Wished he didn't keep sneaking glances to see what he was doing.

Wished the answer was something besides *watching Zach.*

He was clearly listening as Zach filled Alexei in on school and his season, and for the life of him, Zach couldn't imagine why he cared. He'd left without a backward glance, not a single word in six years, and even if Zach accepted that the breakup had been for the best, it didn't excuse the way Hunter had done it and it didn't give him the right to look so fucking interested now.

Also, how was it fucking possible Hunter looked even better in person than he did on TV? Or in those pictures Zach pored over when he could no longer resist the lure of Google?

Like, seriously, *how dare he?*

At least Zach wasn't completely unprepared for how thick Hunter's shoulders were now. Or how his hair had darkened to a deeper blond that made his pale hazel eyes stand out even more. Or how his arms and chest filled out his ridiculously tight V-neck sweater that looked so soft it had to be cashmere.

Zach loved cashmere, damn it. And that was the only reason he wanted to rub his face over the bulge of Hunter's pecs.

The. Only. Reason.

God, it would be so much easier if Hunter weren't so hot.

"What are you doing?"

Zach yanked his gaze away from Hunter and blinked innocently —he hoped—at Barnaby. "I'm helping Alexei chop vegetables." Zach followed Barnaby's gaze to the counter and discovered he'd minced the pepper so thoroughly he'd almost reduced it to paste. *Oops.*

He shoved the pile to one side and picked up the next pepper, swearing he'd pay more attention to what he was doing and not... well, *who* he used to do.

Ugh. That came with images and memories that made Zach's whole body go hot.

Barnaby glanced in Hunter's direction. "You want to talk about it?"

"I can't." He wanted to. God, how he wanted to, no matter how painful rehashing the whole thing would be. But once he started, there'd be no stopping him.

And since Hunter was frequently photographed with gorgeous women on his arm in those stupid pictures Zach should absolutely *not* have Googled, he was certain Hunter would thank him for keeping his mouth shut.

That right there was one of the worst parts of it all. They'd been afraid to tell anyone about their relationship when they'd been kids. And now, even though Zach was out and had been for years, he still could never tell anyone the name of the boy who'd helped him figure it all out. The sweet, patient, beautiful boy who'd made it feel easy.

"Okay, Zachary, I think you need a different job than mutilating my peppers," Alexei announced, prying the knife from Zach's fingers.

Shit. Zach grimaced at what was left on the chopping block. "You didn't want them minced, did you?"

"That does make it harder to put them in the dip," Alexei agreed, gesturing at the platter in front of them.

Zach sighed. "I'm sorry. I'm not myself. Maybe I should—"

"No!" Callum and Barnaby said in unison.

They shared a look, then Barnaby said, "We'd really love for you to stay."

Callum nodded like he was super invested in the idea of a random stranger crashing his Christmas Eve.

Zach smiled weakly, because Callum Morrison was making eye contact and it was freaking him out. "Okay. What else can I do to help?"

"Maybe something that doesn't require a knife?" Barnaby suggested.

"I have just the thing," Alexei said, handing Zach a potato masher.

Zach laughed and happily turned his attention to beating the ever-loving shit out of the massive pot of boiled potatoes. It was extremely satisfying. Barnaby stayed close, chatting about the upcoming semester and plans for the rest of their break while he helped transfer food to the serving dishes. By the time Alexei came to add butter and cream, Zach's arm was tired, and he hadn't looked over at Hunter in at least five minutes.

He could totally do this. He would sit at the opposite end of the table from Hunter, enjoy a nice meal with nice people—one of whom happened to be his hero—then help clean up and go home.

No problem.

3

It was absolutely a problem.

Zach was pretty sure the entire Morrison-Smythe-Belov-Birtwistle-etc. clan was trying to kill him.

His plan worked perfectly while he was tucked in the kitchen helping Alexei and ignoring Hunter for all he was worth. Then he helped carry food to the table, which practically groaned under the weight of the massive feast. Hunter jumped in to help, too, but there was plenty to do, and Zach turned his attention to getting Eleanor into her booster seat and grabbing a couple of beers for himself and Travis.

That last task, though, might have been his fatal mistake because when he turned back to the table, every seat was taken but one.

The one right next to Hunter.

And sure, it could have been a coincidence, or monumentally bad luck, but since no one seemed inclined to make eye contact with Zach as he walked back to the table, he had his doubts.

But it was fine. He could do this. So what if the brush of Hunter's shoulder as he slid into his seat made something in him want to curl up and die? Or that the way their legs bumped made Zach want to scream at the top of his lungs?

Travis didn't know Zach well enough to recognize he was a man on the verge and reached for his beer. Zach considered holding it hostage, since he might need both—at least. He relinquished it only because the idea of making a spectacle of himself was even more horrifying than having to digest food in Hunter Michaelson's presence.

Barnaby's pleased grin slowly dissolved into a concerned frown as he studied Zach's face.

The meal was delicious, at least, and made it easier to ignore Barnaby's worried glances and the way Callum kept looking between Zach and Hunter with a delighted grin. Zach couldn't imagine why Callum seemed so pleased or why Hunter kept glaring at him.

Fortunately, distractions were plentiful with so many people around the table. Eleanor, in particular, was a delight and Zach fell a little bit in love. She was happy to give him big smiles in exchange for his help loading up her plate or cutting her food. He focused on her as much as he could and pretended he couldn't feel Hunter's presence all down the right side of his body like a blow torch.

He just had to last an hour or two, then this would all be a memory. One he would review in minute detail, overthink, and generally give far too much energy—but safely in the past.

Did he need to learn that Hunter had changed his cologne? Nope.

Did the hint of musk and pine make Zach want to shove his face in the crook of Hunter's neck and live there for a week? Yup.

Did it matter? Absolutely not.

Through grim determination, Zach made conversation and enjoyed himself through the meal.

And dessert.

And coffee.

And Jesus *fuck*, how could these people be so nice and social and clearly have way better interpersonal skills than Zach but still not see he was dying inside? The only consolation was that other than thanking him for passing the salt, Hunter didn't try to talk to him.

Though Zach suspected Hunter was as aware of Zach as he was of Hunter. When Zach was talking, Hunter was totally dialed into what he was saying. When Zach's shyness got the better of him and he went quiet, Hunter glanced at him with obvious concern.

Zach wanted to snap at him to knock it the fuck off, but yelling at someone for being polite was probably rude. Right? And that was all this was—Hunter displaying good manners. He didn't know Zach anymore. And Zach didn't know him. Both of these things were by Hunter's choice, and the fact that he was still sexy and smelled good and Zach's dick got a little hard every time their knees bumped didn't mean shit.

The meal finally ended, and Zach leaped from his chair to assist with the cleanup. Hunter helped, too, and Zach decided *fuck it*, meeting Hunter's gaze every time they passed each other between the kitchen and the table. If Hunter was going to look, then why not look back? Why not make this as weird and uncomfortable as humanly possible?

Zach swallowed back the hysterical laughter bubbling up in his throat.

Just as he finished clearing the table, Barnaby called him over near the door, where he and Travis each held a file box.

"I found all the stuff for Sorenson's class. I'm sorry it's a bit jumbled together."

Zach lifted the lid off the box Travis held. Inside was a treasure trove of books, binders, and reams of loose papers clipped together. "Wow."

"I held on to everything in case he asked me to TA the class again. And you know how Dr. Sorenson sometimes goes on tangents, so there are handwritten notes on the presentation print-outs that I think you'll find helpful. Also, I annotated the books we read in class, and I thought you might like to have those as well?"

"Yes, please. Thank you," Zach said eagerly, happy to have anything Barnaby thought would help. The only problem was this was *a lot* of stuff.

Before he could suggest he'd have to make two trips or go get his car, Callum clapped him on the shoulder. "You can't carry all that."

"Well, I—"

"Hunter! You're headed out, right?"

Hunter looked up from the sink, his arms in soap suds to the elbow. He and Callum exchanged a look and suddenly Hunter was drying his hands and rolling his sleeves back down on the way to join their little group.

"Yeah, I should get going." It almost sounded like a question.

"Great, perfect timing," Callum said. "Can you help Zach carry this stuff?"

"Of course." Hunter took the box from Travis without looking at Zach.

Barnaby shoved the second box into Zach's arms with enthusiasm.

Zach frowned at his friend and mouthed, *I'm going to get you for this*, satisfied when Barnaby's eyes widened with alarm.

Before Zach could lob more threats, Callum held out Hunter's and Zach's coats. For a moment, it looked as though Hunter would rather brave the bitter New Brunswick night without outerwear than relinquish his box, but, after a brief struggle, Callum managed to pry it from Hunter's grasp. Hunter threw on a wool coat that practically screamed *bespoke* and snatched the box back.

How could such a bulky article of clothing complement a man's ass like that? Then again, this particular hockey butt had trended on Twitter. More than once.

#bubblehunter

God, it had been beautiful and big and round in high school, but now it was so—

"Thank you for coming tonight," Callum said, startling Zach just as Barnaby thrust his box of coursework back into Zach's hands.

Callum gave Hunter a side hug and steered him toward the door Travis held open.

Zach remembered his manners at the last minute, thanking Rupert and Callum for having him over, and promising to be in touch with Barnaby—oh, would he ever—and Alexei.

Everyone called out their goodnights, then the door shut and

Zach was trapped in the quiet hallway with only Hunter for company.

How the fuck had they gotten here?

What followed was the longest, most awkward, dead silent elevator ride in history. The stupid thing was huge, but they stood side by side, facing the door, close enough that Hunter's goddamn cologne teased Zach's nose.

They crossed the massive empty space on the first floor accompanied only by the sounds of their footsteps, then Zach led the way through the door and out into the bracingly cold air. He wondered if he could make it all the way home with the Ghost of Sex-Lives Past floating behind him, blessedly silent.

But then Zach had never been that lucky.

Hunter cleared his throat. "So, how've you been?"

Zach turned slowly, his eyebrows all the way up. Because...*really*?

"Look, I know I'm probably the last person you wanted to see." Hunter licked his lips and swallowed hard and Zach wished he didn't remember the taste of Hunter's kiss or his skin, especially just there over his Adam's apple. "And I know you're justifiably mad at me, but —I mean— for what it's worth, it's really good to see you."

Zach looked at Hunter like there was something seriously fucking wrong with him, and it was no less than he deserved.

Hell, he was getting off easy.

He'd tried to give Zach space while they were around all those people, particularly since Zach didn't know Callum or Rupert and it was their house. Hunter hadn't wanted to make things any more awkward than they already were and the Zach he'd known had *hated* to be embarrassed. Not that anyone loved it, but for Zach it was less about feeling foolish and more about being made the focus of that kind of attention.

But now they were on their own, and Hunter wanted to know more. He wanted to know Zach was doing okay. He wanted to know *Zach*. He had no right to expect anything more than a brush-off, but he hoped. He'd been hoping since the moment he'd laid eyes on Zach again.

When Zach turned away and strode down the street without saying a word, Hunter jogged after him, no less determined as they weaved their way around pedestrians and strode past closed shops, cheerful restaurants, and boisterous bars bursting with people still out celebrating.

When he caught up to Zach and snuck a peek at his face, he expected to find anger—and Zach did look annoyed—but mostly he looked confused.

Hunter could work with that. He confused people all the time. "Are we walking all the way to your house?"

Zach glanced over at him. "What?"

Hunter hefted the box he carried, getting a better grip. "I'm game, but your house is, like, four miles away, it's negative eight degrees, and my car is parked back at Callum's, so…"

"Oh. Ah, no." Zach did something that almost passed for a laugh and Hunter felt like he'd just scored the sweetest goal ever. "Mom and Dad are in the Caymans now."

"And you didn't go with them?"

Zach frowned at him. "I'm still in school."

Hunter was confused. "Don't you have a winter break?"

"*Oh.* No, I mean—" Zach laughed for real this time and Hunter manfully resisted doing a victory dance. "Yeah, sorry. Mom and Dad moved to the Caymans last year. I live on my own. Here."

Zach stopped by a door tucked between two shop windows and Hunter realized Zach meant *here* literally.

Hunter felt a flutter of panic in his chest. *Damn it.* He was out of time already. He didn't want to say goodbye. Not yet.

Zach propped his box on his hip and dug a hand into his pocket, presumably searching for a key. Hunter had to drag his eyes away from that process—god, those jeans fit him like a dream—and didn't see Zach's box slipping from his grasp until it was too late.

Hunter's desperate attempt to catch it only made things worse, the lid popping off as the box tipped and crashed to the sidewalk.

Hunter's heart stopped as papers and books cascaded across the wet, snowy concrete.

"*Shit!*" Zach shouted, his keys clattering on the ground as he reached for the box and tried to shovel the contents back inside. Hunter hurried to help, balancing his box on his knee to keep it dry while quickly extricating loose sheets of paper and a copy of *Jane Eyre* from the snowbank separating the sidewalk from the street.

"Shit, shit, *shit*," Zach muttered, attempting to arrange wet pages in a way that wouldn't damage the dry ones.

"Here, if I take some of those," Hunter suggested, spreading wet papers on the top of his box and under his elbow, "they won't stick together so much. We need something to dry them with, though. The sooner the better." Zach seemed to agree and leaped to his feet. Hunter followed suit and pressed Zach's keys into his hand.

Zach had the door unlocked and open before he hesitated. Hunter held his breath while Zach's gaze darted between Hunter's face and the papers going translucent with melting snow. Hunter bit back a promise to leave as soon as the box was delivered. The universe had offered him this opportunity and he wasn't going to throw it away.

Finally, Zach led the way through the door and jogged up the stairs, Hunter trailing behind and trying not to enjoy the view too much.

He failed so hard his mouth watered.

The single door at the landing led into a small one-bedroom apartment. Hunter immediately recognized the living and dining room furniture from Zach's parents' house. The large pieces were pushed against walls and took up most of the tight space, but Hunter could see why Zach wouldn't want to part with them. The red plaid couch probably didn't fit the typical Cayman Islands aesthetic, but it looked right at home in Zach's eclectic jumble of a home.

Hunter had a lot of happy memories associated with that couch, including giving his first blow job. He wondered if Zach still had the same bed. He shivered. Talk about happy memories.

Shucking his coat, Zach tossed it on a dining room chair and started arranging papers and books on the table and the postage-stamp-sized kitchen counter.

Hunter moved more slowly, trying not to attract attention as he carefully folded his coat over the back of a chair. When Zach didn't ask him what the fuck he thought he was doing and boot him out onto the street, he did a teeny mental fist pump and reached for a wad of paper towels.

They worked quickly, Hunter bent over the table blotting up water from the wettest documents and books while Zach's long fingers danced over the pages as he spread them out. He had always loved Zach's hands—and not just because those fingers could reach all kinds of interesting places. They were strong and quick and constantly in motion when he spoke, their movements increasingly animated as Zach's passion on a subject rose. Combined with his keen eye and powerful brain, it was no wonder he was an exceptional goalie.

But the strongest memories Hunter held of Zach's hands were the moments they'd been still. Holding Hunter's hand beneath the blanket while they watched a movie with one of their families or beneath their coats on the bus to a game. Spread across Hunter's stomach or chest when Zach was curled up behind him.

Those hands, and Zach, had made it safe for Hunter to ask for things he'd never dared to ask for before.

Seeing Zach's broad shoulders bent over the counter, those fucking capable hands working gently with Barnaby's handwritten notes, Hunter remembered the past. He remembered how his agent, his parents, and his coaches had prepared him for the draft, for the big leagues, while only Zach had made him feel like it was okay to want more. He could play hockey all day and get media training after that and still come back to Zach's room and know Zach would wrap his long arms and strong legs around Hunter and hold on.

Of the two of them, people had always assumed Hunter was the toughest. The strongest. But he wasn't. He hadn't been back then, either.

That had always been Zach.

Zach stood up and cracked his neck, surveying Barnaby's papers, then froze as if surprised to find Hunter there. They'd both ended up in the tiny kitchen, which was barely big enough to hold them, but Zach didn't back away.

Hunter barely breathed.

Denial was a powerful force, and it was crushing to realize that for six years he'd managed to convince himself that he was okay. That he hadn't wanted to come back and find Zach. That he'd made the right choice.

That he had no regrets.

It had all been a lie. It had to be because just seeing Zach again set something right in Hunter that he hadn't realized was out of place. It filled a gap in his soul.

He wanted to tell Zach that, but he was out of practice when it came to making himself vulnerable. Zach was the only one he'd been able to trust with that kind of honesty and the soft, infinitely bruisable parts Hunter kept hidden. No one since had come close.

Of course, Zach probably wouldn't want to hear it anyway. Hunter had destroyed what they once had, and now his courage was in ruins, too.

So he stared into those dark brown eyes he'd refused to admit he'd missed so much, his chest aching like someone squeezed his heart in their fist, and wished there was a way to undo the past.

Zach stared back and tilted his head, his expression curious. Hunter didn't see Zach lift a hand until his fingertips brushed over Hunter's cheekbone.

The air caught in Hunter's throat and he stood stock-still until those long, elegant fingers cupped his cheek. Then he let his eyes drift closed and nuzzled his cheek into Zach's palm, grateful to be given what he didn't deserve and selfish enough to take it anyway.

4

Touching Hunter was a spectacularly terrible idea.

Zach told himself it was just curiosity, but that didn't explain the arousal heating his blood. The memories had faded over the years, but for a long time Hunter had been the measuring stick by which all other men had been judged, at least when it came to sex. Now he wanted to know if he'd imagined how good it had been.

They'd been kids. Inexperienced ones, at that. There was every reason to think this could lead to spectacularly mediocre sex. Hell, Zach hoped it did. Maybe *that* would be the final nail in the coffin, sealing away his feelings for Hunter. God knew, it would be nice to be able to keep that stupid lid shut.

Then he brushed his lips over Hunter's and knew he was fucked. If anything got nailed tonight, it wasn't going to be that goddamn coffin.

An urgent sound rose from Hunter's throat as he leaned into Zach, for all the world looking and sounding as eager and innocent as Zach remembered from high school. It shook him to think Hunter might be unchanged in some way. In *this* way. And even more shocking was how much Zach wanted it to be true.

He clutched a fistful of Hunter's sweater, crushing the luxurious cashmere, and tugged Hunter closer. He came easily, his hands on Zach's hips. Zach had worked so hard to forget this, to pretend Hunter hadn't been capable of being this sweet. This giving.

But he had been. And while the overwhelming emotions Zach had felt for this man weren't present any longer, their echoes were, like ghosts rising up to remind him of what he'd lost. *Who* he'd lost.

And why Hunter had been so fucking impossible to forget.

With another hungry sound, Hunter's lips parted and Zach slid his tongue between them, falling into the kiss. It was as easy as riding a bike—years without and he knew just what to do. He reveled in the stroke of Hunter's tongue and the way he melted against Zach. As easy as breathing, Zach wrapped his arms around Hunter and held him up.

The whiplash lean kid had become a man of heavy muscles and thick thighs. Hunter used to practically vibrate with the need to move at all times, but now Zach marveled at how steady Hunter felt in his arms. How sure. The power, that *energy*, remained, but calm within a heavier body, anchored inside Hunter's thicker waist and powerful limbs.

Their lips parted and Zach muttered, "You're a goddamn brick shithouse."

Hunter let out a surprised laugh, low and quiet, his lips brushing Zach's cheeks. "I'll take that as a compliment."

"You should." Zach cupped the base of Hunter's skull with a hand and tilted his head for another kiss. Hunter clung to him, grip tight and desperate, and it felt like a victory.

Sliding his hands down, Zach hummed happily when he cupped the huge, round globes of Hunter's ass in his palms. Brick shithouse didn't even begin to cover what was going on back there. He dug his fingers into all that glorious muscle, and slid his thigh between Hunter's, nudging up against his balls.

Hunter groaned and rolled his hips, searching for more pressure. They staggered into the counter and Zach steadied them, holding firm while Hunter ground against him and moaned into their kiss.

Zach's head spun with the feeling of Hunter's erection against his own. He could picture Hunter's cock perfectly. Fondly. Once upon a time, he'd worshipped the thick, heavy shaft roped with veins and topped with a wide, silky cap. He used to tease Hunter about its size, loving how Hunter would blush furiously and insist Zach was being ridiculous.

He tore his mouth from Hunter's, ignoring his groan of protest, and ran the tip of his nose along the crest of one high cheekbone.

"You going to let me see it?" Zach murmured.

Hunter blinked, his gaze vague. "What?"

"Your perfectly perfect dick."

Hunter's cheeks turned pink, the tips of his ears, too. It was fucking adorable and terrible, and Zach didn't know what to do with the feelings it conjured, those ghosts returning to haunt him again.

Taking advantage of Hunter's distraction, he reversed their positions and pinned Hunter's hips against the counter with his hands. The carefully tailored trousers Zach had tried not to ogle earlier didn't just accentuate Hunter's huge butt. His cock strained against the flat front, ruining the lines in ways that ruined Zach right back.

Zach dragged his eyes from that glorious sight to Hunter's flushed face, one kiss-swollen lip caught between his teeth. He was temptation incarnate and Zach wasn't going to try to resist.

"I'm going to blow you now."

Hunter looked a little wild around the eyes, his mouth opening and closing a few times before he managed a flustered, "Okay."

Zach smirked and dropped to his knees, wrestling open Hunter's pants and shoving up his shirt to reveal a taut, perfectly ridged abdomen.

God, how could he be even more beautiful than Zach remembered? The soft-core shirtless calendar some genius in PR had cooked up last season hadn't done him justice. Zach liked to pretend he wasn't picturing Hunter while he jerked off, but now he wasn't even going to be able to lie to himself about it.

He licked over Hunter's belly button and held on when Hunter's stomach jerked in surprise. Grinning, he bit the ridge that ran from

Hunter's hip to his groin, loving how it made Hunter squirm, then kissed his way across to the other side, dragging his chin through the trail of baby-soft blond hair that arrowed from Hunter's navel to his cock. Fingers hooked in Hunter's belt, Zach dragged skin-tight briefs and perfectly tailored pants down those magnificent thighs. He rubbed his face over the coarse hair, digging his teeth into the defined muscles.

Hunter groaned, legs shifting and muscles quivering. His hands shook where they hovered above Zach's head uncertainly. His reactions seemed honest, unpracticed, and Zach wanted to spend hours worshiping Hunter with his teeth and his hands, listening to his gasps and moans while he ignored Hunter's cock.

But that wasn't going to happen. Not tonight. Not ever.

Hunter jerked when Zach pressed his face into Hunter's groin and rubbed against the warm skin just beside Hunter's cock. Zach sucked it between his teeth, left his mark, then kissed a path up and over Hunter's straining dick to leave a mark on the other side.

"You used to be a boxers guy," Zach observed as he finally wrestled the tight briefs to Hunter's knees.

Hunter let out a strangled laugh. "They look weird under these pants."

Zach ran his hands up the back of Hunter's bare thighs and pinched one cheek. "You mean your pants, which you've clearly had tailored to hug every inch of your goddamn ass, are too tight for boxers." He cupped the gorgeous ass in question, soothing the spot he'd tweaked, and groaned against Hunter's flat belly.

Jesus Christ, he was a work of art.

Hunter's knees wobbled. "Zach, I—"

Zach didn't want to hear it—just his name on Hunter's lips, voice cracking, was too much.

Desperate to shut him up, Zach took Hunter's cock all the way down to the root. The huge, fucking perfect crown almost—but not quite—triggered his gag reflex as he swallowed.

"*Zach!*" Hunter cried out in surprise. Hell, he fucking wailed it, and the sound pierced Zach in the chest. Any delusion he had about not feeling too much, not recalling why he'd missed this man, failed spectacularly, but he didn't care. Not when Hunter was threading his fingers into Zach's hair and clenching it in his fist. Not when his panting breaths bottomed out into desperate whimpers.

Zach squeezed his eyes shut and focused on the cock in his mouth and what he was doing to Hunter to the exclusion of all else. Hunter's shaft slid along his tongue, leaving traces of bitter pre-come. He stopped each retreat when the head almost slipped from his mouth, then plunged forward again, taking Hunter all the way down his throat.

Hunter murmured Zach's name, and cursed, and petted his hair when he wasn't almost tearing it out at the roots. Zach didn't let up, going deep and then easing back to suck on the head and pump the shaft, slick from his saliva, with his fist. It was messy and fast.

Perfect.

Hunter stared down at him, the unusually pale hazel of his irises a thin, glowing ring around dark pupils dilated with arousal.

His cock twitched as Zach closed his eyes against the blazing intimacy. The sting of his scalp when Hunter yanked his hair was the only thing grounding him. Hunter wasn't steering, and he wasn't trying to force Zach to do anything, but it was a tangible means to know he was taking the stupid man to pieces.

He'd wanted Hunter to understand what he'd missed, what he would continue to be missing, but it was easy to forget about that when Hunter was putty in his hands. Petty revenge didn't matter when Hunter's thighs trembled. He couldn't dwell on the past when Hunter was gasping for air and groaning his name.

Zach cupped Hunter's balls, finding them high and tight to his body. Hunter was about to come, but Zach wasn't even close to done yet.

He withdrew with a filthy and intentional slurp that might have embarrassed him if Hunter's eyes didn't glaze over with lust at the sound. He knew what Hunter liked.

"God, Zach. Where did you learn to do that?"

"You're not the only person I've ever done that with anymore."

Something flitted across Hunter's face. Something Zach was certain would piss him off if Hunter gave voice to it.

Zach stood, knees cracking. His cock ached from being jammed to one side in his jeans but he ignored it. He grabbed Hunter's waistband, having to work a little to haul the tight fabric back over the most maximus gluteus ever.

Fuck, Zach wanted him so bad it hurt.

"Come on," he said, taking Hunter's hand.

Hunter's eyes widened but Zach wasn't going to ask why. Surprise? Delight? Trepidation? Tomorrow, Zach would overanalyze every moment, trying to determine what each of Hunter's words or gestures had meant, but right now Zach was going to do something he never allowed himself to do.

He was going to think with his dick.

How Hunter Michaelson, of all people, made that feel like a safe thing to do was something Zach could spend far too much time mulling over later.

Towing Hunter into his bedroom, he barely paused to turn on the small lamp beside the bed and kick the door shut behind them. He ran his hands over Hunter's chest, shoving his shirt and sweater up and off to map Hunter's broad pecs. He turned until Hunter's legs were pinned against the bed.

Hunter leaned back, letting Zach look his fill, his incredible core strength holding him steady at an angle above the mattress.

Zach traced his fingers over Hunter's tight, delineated abs, because he was weak and who the fuck could resist? Then he dragged his eyes up Hunter's torso and met his gaze.

Hunter's body might have all new topography to explore, but his face was still as expressive, as easy for Zach to read, as ever. The flush meant Hunter was turned on and that bright light in his eyes meant he was eager for whatever came next.

Zach pulled him in and kissed him again, running his hands everywhere he could reach. He marveled at so much smooth, warm skin, delighted Hunter still had almost no chest hair.

With barely a nudge of encouragement, Hunter fell back on the bed. He was unbelievably sexy sprawled out across Zach's dark sheets and Zach shuddered thinking about how much better he'd look completely naked.

Hunter must have read his mind because he shucked his pants so quickly it was lucky they didn't tear. Zach followed suit, stripping in a matter of seconds while Hunter propped himself up on his elbows to watch.

Who wouldn't be turned on by being looked at like that? By being *desired* like that? Zach crawled onto the bed and over Hunter, who lay still, his cheeks flushed and his pale eyes wide, appearing content for Zach to do as he pleased.

Zach wanted to eat him alive.

He settled for a kiss. One that was supposed to be quick and filthy and instead melted into something else altogether. Their tongues danced between their mouths, their lips making slick sounds as they parted, only briefly, before diving in for more.

Zach didn't dare lower his body onto Hunter for fear he'd go off the moment they touched. Hunter's legs moved restlessly along the insides of Zach's thighs, the occasional brush of their cocks eliciting long moans from them both.

Hunter's hands coasted over Zach's shoulders and down his back and ribs, over and over, leaving warmth in their wake. The light touch should have tickled, but Zach was too far gone, the need pounding at him.

Hunter clenched a fist in Zach's hair and yanked, ending the kiss. "*Please*, Zach."

A shiver worked down Zach's back at Hunter's hoarse plea. "Please what?"

Hunter's other hand locked into Zach's hair, making it impossible for Zach to look anywhere but into Hunter's pale eyes.

"Please fuck me."

THIS WAS NOT how tonight was supposed to go.

Then again, Hunter wasn't supposed to be here at all. Not that he didn't want to be. Not that he was sorry it was happening this way. Not that he didn't want Zach with every fiber of his being. But a teeny little alarm in the back of his head warned him this was an epically bad idea.

He was supposed to be at Callum's house, drinking coffee or beer and declaring he was going to learn from Callum's example and live a more honest, open life.

Then again, this did feel pretty goddamn honest.

"*Please*," he begged, hoping his grip on Zach's hair disguised the way his hands shook.

Zach nodded and yanked his bedside drawer open.

A condom and a bottle of lube hit the mattress by Hunter's hip, and for half a second he wondered about the condom, like it was still high school. Like Zach hadn't just told Hunter he was no longer the only man Zach had been with.

Hunter could have guessed as much without being told. Zach had a new and unmistakable confidence. They'd been bumbling kids the first time they'd hooked up, and even at the end, after all that practice, Zach hadn't had these kinds of moves.

Deep throating? Until five minutes ago, Hunter had been eighty percent certain that only happened in porn.

Zach ran his hands down Hunter's chest with a hungry look, his thumbnails flicking Hunter's nipples. Hunter arched up to get more of that sting and Zach obliged while his eyes continued roaming. There was no mistaking the appreciation in his gaze.

For the first time in a long time, maybe ever in his adult life, Hunter was proud of his body in a context that wasn't hockey.

If he hadn't been at Callum's and seen Zach being the same charmingly shy man Hunter knew and luuh—liked a lot, he would have thought Zach had conquered his social anxieties entirely to see him now.

The combination, though, was kryptonite to Hunter.

He tried to draw Zach down into another kiss, but Zach wasn't having it. The little smirk on his lips made even more blood flow into Hunter's already achingly hard cock. He sucked in a shaky breath when Zach dipped down to pull one of Hunter's nipples into his warm, wet mouth.

Pleasure arched from his chest to his cock where it lay on his belly. Hunter reveled in it, gasping for more. He hadn't been celibate in the years since high school but he *had* tried to convince himself he'd imagined that the need, and his desire, could be this consuming.

Zach's tongue dipped into his belly button and he jerked, his stomach muscles tensing and making his cock bounce off Zach's chin. The impact was an electric shock to Hunter's system. He groaned and writhed beneath Zach's mouth, desperate for more, his hands running through Zach's messy curls. Zach didn't give him even a second to catch his breath, his lips circling the head of Hunter's cock and sucking hard.

Hunter's hips lifted off the bed of their own accord and his flailing arms sent half the pillows over the side of the bed before he locked a hand around the headboard.

Zach's mouth was heaven, his dark brown eyes molten as they watched Hunter's face to see how thoroughly he wrecked Hunter.

Hunter stared back, so lost in Zach's gaze that he was shocked by the brush of cool, wet fingers behind his balls.

He pulled his legs up—why bother with any pretense?—and his cock slipped from Zach's mouth. Zach's eyes made another hungry trip over Hunter's body before coming back to his face.

Hunter had never made so much eye contact in his life, let alone while in bed. He wasn't sure he liked it, even if he couldn't seem to stop. He felt vulnerable and young and inexperienced all over again, and yet it still felt like a loss when Zach looked down to where his fingers traced the seam of skin that ran from behind Hunter's balls to his hole. Zach circled his entrance and Hunter's entire existence narrowed down to that one spot. His breath hitched with a helpless sound when Zach slid one finger past the tight ring of muscle. It felt good, but not as good as Zach's long, low groan at how Hunter's body gave in to him easily. Zach thrust the finger in and out, testing the muscle and judging when Hunter could take a second.

Hunter moaned, unembarrassed by his body's eager reception. If he'd had any access to the higher brain function necessary to form words, he would have told Zach how he liked to do this to himself. He would have gladly confessed to his secret stash of plugs and silicone cocks and a wildly overpriced brand of lube—*worth it!*—back in Pittsburgh and how he indulged himself when he had a rare quiet night at home.

Or maybe Zach could guess. He spread his fingers, opening Hunter up, and Hunter's muscles gave and gave again. His spine felt liquified, and he rode on waves of pleasure, all heightened without the frustrations inherent in fingering or fucking himself.

Then Zach's fingers brushed Hunter's prostate, and ecstasy rushed through him like a symphony when all he'd been doing for years was humming his favorite song. He was lost, his body singing arias.

He staved off his orgasm by clamping the hand not fastened to the headboard around his cock. He didn't want this to be over. Not yet.

When the blood thrumming in Hunter's ears faded a little, he discovered Zach was muttering a string of curses mixed with detailed, if exasperated, observations about Hunter's cock and ass. Hunter smiled, eyes closed, too aroused to care how big his ass was and whether that was a good or bad thing.

Then Zach's fingers were gone and Hunter snapped his eyes open to see Zach reaching for the condom with an unsteady hand. Of course, he still managed to get it on quickly and confidently and like his hands weren't shaking at all.

Fucking goalies.

Before Hunter could dwell in the overwhelming happiness such a simple thing could provoke, Zach crawled over him, his expression determined. Not like this was a chore, but like he couldn't wait another second to be inside Hunter. He hooked an arm beneath one of Hunter's knees, the head of his cock teasing a trail of lube across Hunter's ass before settling against his hole.

Hunter met Zach's hot, dark gaze and answered the question before it was asked.

"Yes."

Without looking away, Zach pushed in, his brows furrowing when Hunter's muscles didn't cooperate and tried to keep him out. Zach bit his lower lip and leaned closer, pushing a little harder. He was totally focused and Hunter couldn't help but smile at the familiar look of concentration.

He clamped a hand around the back of Zach's neck, met him stare for stare, and let go a long breath.

Zach's cock popped inside.

Fuck.

How could Hunter have forgotten the intimacy of letting this man into his body? He wanted to squeeze his eyes shut and hide. To somehow be invulnerable to his own needs and his desire for Zach. Instead, he couldn't look away, buzzing with the stretch—which was perfect—and the sting he craved as much as the pleasure he knew would follow on their heels.

He arched, groaning happily as Zach thrust forward, relentless. The burn gave way to a fullness no silicone dick had ever managed, no matter the size. Zach took what Hunter so willingly gave until Zach's hips were flush to Hunter's ass.

"Please, Zach." He was beyond caring what he sounded like. "*Move.*"

Zach nodded, his eyes dropping to where they were connected. He withdrew slowly, his shaft running along singing nerves until the head caught on Hunter's rim. Hunter gasped but Zach seemed utterly mesmerized by what he saw.

Hunter didn't even try to look. He'd come in an instant.

Hell, he almost came when Zach pushed back in, nailing Hunter's prostate on the first goddamn try. The symphony exploded to life inside Hunter again.

By the third thrust, their bodies met with enough force to shake the bed against the wall, though Hunter was only dimly aware of the noise. He held on to the headboard for dear life and stared up at Zach through unseeing eyes, each thump of their bodies making him cry out.

God, it was just *so fucking good.*

He begged for more. And Zach gave it to him.

The hand Hunter had wrapped around the back of Zach's neck slipped on hot, slick skin. He tugged, drawing Zach closer, until their mouths met in an uncoordinated, teeth-clacking kiss. Zach shifted, bending Hunter until his knees were practically by his ears, and the kiss got far less messy—unless Hunter counted what it was doing to his head and heart.

He thrust his tongue against Zach's and acknowledged that he'd been lying to himself for the last three months. Hell, for the last six years.

God, he had regrets. *Of course,* he had fucking regrets.

He'd given up *this.*

Hunter kissed Zach and tried to pour how much he'd missed him into every parry of their tongues. He knew he should use his words, but goddamn, it was hard to come up with any when Zach was fucking him hard and fast, their bodies moving together like they'd never so much as skipped a beat.

Zach used to revel in making Hunter come untouched, and Hunter had spent the last six years assuming that had only been possible because of his age and the sheer horniness that came with being eighteen.

Turned out, he was an idiot.

He didn't need anything but Zach to get there, because Zach knew how to work Hunter over like he'd been given an instruction manual.

Fuck, who was Hunter kidding? Zach had *written* the fucking instruction manual.

And as if he'd just flipped to the section on making Hunter come so hard he cried, Zach broke their kiss and leaned back, gripping Hunter's hips in his long fingers. Hunter gasped, knowing what would happen next and suddenly overwhelmed by the prospect. Zach switched to rapid, shallow thrusts that glanced off Hunter's prostate like Zach's dick came with a compass and Hunter's prostate was true north.

The noise that tore out of Hunter's throat was too loud to be called a groan and—he sincerely hoped—too deep to be a scream. It seemed to go on forever until, back arching, his orgasm tore through him, curling his toes and whiting out his brain.

Zach didn't let up until Hunter's dick—hell, his whole body—was twitching weakly. Then Zach thrust deep, wrapping his arms around Hunter as he bucked hard once, twice, then froze, shaking, above him.

Hunter held him close and floated in blissed-out contentment.

The moment Zach took his first deep breath, it was as though their strings had been cut. They slumped to the bed, Hunter's legs aching as he unfolded, his ass deliciously sore as Zach slid from him.

Fuck. Hunter was exhausted.

Not from the incredible sex, or long day, or tough season, or any of the other reasons that would have made perfect sense.

No, he was exhausted from years of pretending he didn't want this. *Need* this.

He curled up on his side and closed his eyes, trying not to flinch when Zach slid from the bed rather than settling down beside him. Hunter should get up, get dressed, and leave, but before he could convince himself to do it, Zach pulled the heavy flannel sheets and comforter up over him. Hunter murmured something nonsensical that probably conveyed his surprise but hopefully also sounded pleased. The apartment was actually pretty chilly when he wasn't on fire for Zach. Or because of Zach. Or whatever the hell had just happened.

Hunter tried to gather his wits so he could figure out how to extricate himself from the bed and what he feared would become an awkward situation.

And promptly passed out.

He startled awake when Zach gently drew a soft towel between his cheeks and over his stomach, wiping away the worst of the lube. Hunter's eyes closed again as soon as Zach was done but managed to stay awake long enough to roll over and catch Zach's arm, towing him under the covers and into the warm cocoon his body had created.

Hunter burrowed against Zach's chest shamelessly, silently begging for comfort for which he had no right to ask.

Zach hesitated, then folded his arms around Hunter and pulled him in closer.

Something gave in Hunter's chest. Something new and hopeful mixed with a feeling he could only describe as grief. He took comfort from the familiar scent of Zach's skin and felt the prickle of tears as Zach's hands rubbed up and down his back.

There was a lot to say. A lot to think about.

Hunter didn't know where to start, but he hid his face against Zach's chest and admitted, "You're still the only person I've ever done that with."

Zach didn't say anything, but he held Hunter tighter and tangled their legs together, which was the best answer Hunter could hope to get.

ZACH KNEW he shouldn't fall asleep with Hunter. Hell, he shouldn't be under the covers, wrapped around Hunter at all. It definitely wasn't cute, or charming, and under no circumstances should it make Zach's heart ache that Hunter still needed this time after having sex. He'd always clung to Zach like a limpet, and Zach had always loved it.

He used to think it meant more than it did, and maybe that was one of the reasons he'd been so shocked to be ditched without a word, forgotten.

But then again, maybe he hadn't been forgotten at all.

Not that it mattered. Zach didn't know what Hunter wanted—and he didn't think Hunter knew either—but he wasn't a dumb kid anymore. He wouldn't read too much into any of it.

Zach's eyes slipped closed without his permission and he buried his nose in Hunter's hair, swearing he'd get up and send Hunter packing in a minute.

Hours later, a stray beam of sunlight snuck through Zach's poorly drawn curtains and woke him up.

He was hardly surprised to find himself alone.

It still stung, though.

Motherfucker.

Zach rolled over, turning his back on the window and the empty bed where Hunter had been, and pretended there was some comfort in knowing all along that hooking up with Hunter Michaelson would be a terrible fucking idea.

5

Hunter was, once again, ruminating on life. He lay stretched out on his couch and stared up at the freshly plastered ceiling of his living room. He'd gotten home from practice an hour ago and turned on HGTV in an attempt to distract himself from doing this very thing, but of course it hadn't worked.

So he studied the swirls of paint and plaster and contemplated his existence. He was getting to be something of a pro at it, and the only reason it was a problem was because he'd been doing almost nothing but this or hockey for the better part of two weeks.

Even his cat couldn't deal with him anymore. She sat on the coffee table, fluffy tail swishing back and forth, blue eyes judging.

Sighing, he picked up his phone from where it had been vibrating, ignored, on his chest. He opened the text app, bypassing the unread messages waiting for him. His fingers hovered over the keyboard. Then he decided, if he was going to do this, he was going to be an adult and face the music properly.

He dialed Callum's number.

"Hey, kid! What's up?"

"I fucked up."

There was a pause. "Do you need to call your agent before you tell me what's going on?"

"What?" Hunter jolted upright. Just the suggestion that shit had gone that far off the rails was enough to pump him full of adrenaline. Then he collapsed back on the couch and laughed. "Jesus, *no*. Nothing that bad."

Callum let out a loud, relieved breath. "Okay, you scared me for a second. So, what's going on?"

Hunter licked his lips and steeled himself. He wished he'd gotten around to finishing the conversation with Callum at Christmastime, but what had seemed almost impossible to say then was nothing compared to the confession he needed to make today.

"I'm gay," he started, then paused, trying to figure out a good way to spin the next part so he didn't come across as a total douchebag.

"Super," Callum said.

Hunter blinked at his ceiling, then snorted. "That's it? *Super?*"

"Well, thank you for trusting me. I hope you know I'll support you any way I can."

Hunter swallowed past the unexpected lump in his throat. "Thanks."

Callum gave him a moment to collect himself. "You okay?"

"I am." Hunter took a deep breath. "You don't seem surprised."

"Do you want me to pretend I'm surprised?" Callum asked. "Because I can do that."

Hunter huffed, exasperated. "No, I don't want you to pretend."

"Good, because I have to be honest with you—at eighteen, you weren't very good at not staring at Mitch's ass when he paraded around the locker room naked."

"Which was *all the fucking time*," Hunter said defensively.

"Hey! I'm not saying I blame you, or even that you were alone, I'm just saying you weren't subtle." Callum laughed, then in a more serious tone added, "Also, there was the whole thing where you couldn't stop making big, sad moon eyes at Zach when you had dinner with us a couple of weeks ago."

Hunter sighed. "Yeah. That's the part where I fucked up."

"No one who was here will say anything to anyone."

"I'm not worried about that," Hunter said, waving it aside even though Callum couldn't see him. "It's just that, after I bumped into Zach at your house, I walked him home and...then, I uh...bumped into him a whole lot more."

Callum let out an amused snort. "Really? That's what you're going with?"

"Shut up."

"No," Callum replied cheerfully. "So, what's the problem? Was it bad? Did you leave him hanging? You'll never convince me that sweet kid is going to out you or made a recording or something."

"No, no, nothing like that. It was...it was great, honestly. Like, *really* great. He was amazing. He's super fit and, uh, has definitely learned a thing or two, and I—"

"Ooookay. Thank you. I do *not* need the details," Callum said. "We can just leave it that it was good."

"It was, until..." Hunter faded off, ashamed to admit to the rest.

"Until?" Callum prompted.

"Until I woke up at dawn and left without leaving a note or waking him up," Hunter said in a rush.

"*Dude.*"

Hunter cringed at the disappointment in Callum's voice.

"*I know.*" Hunter was beyond being embarrassed by his plaintive wail. "It was totally *not* what I was going to do, but I woke up and it was Christmas Day, and I was supposed to be home with my family and had forty texts from my mother saying I had better be dead because that was the only excuse for not coming home on Christmas Eve and she was going to call the police to search for me. So I got dressed and Zach was still totally zonked out and he looked so sweet, and I had no fucking idea what I was supposed to say or do or what he wanted."

"Oh boy," Callum muttered.

"So I left, and I swear my plan was to send him a text to explain and to apologize for taking off."

"Okay, not a great plan, but that doesn't sound terrible."

"Except I forgot to make sure I had his number."

There was a long silence. "Okay, wow. You totally fucked up."

"I did." Hunter shut his eyes. "I really did."

"So, what are you going to do about it?" Callum asked in his best dad voice.

"Think about nothing else for two weeks, then call you to whine?"

"How's that working out?" God, Callum's dad voice apparently had levels.

"Not great. But I was thinking, well…" Hunter trailed off because this was the part he'd been dreading almost as much as telling Callum what an asshole he'd been in the first place. "I was hoping you might help me."

"How so?" Callum asked suspiciously.

"I need Zach's number. I Googled him, but I couldn't find a way to get in touch with him that isn't through his school, which doesn't seem like the right place for me to call and grovel."

"That would be uncool," Callum agreed.

Hunter sat up on the couch and shut off the TV, relieved to finally be doing something other than stewing in his guilt. "So…I was hoping you might be able to get his number? Maybe from Barnaby?"

"Are we in middle school?"

Hunter cringed. "Would you rather pass him a note for me? Because short of these two options, the best I can do is hope to get his address right and send him a letter like we live in the Victorian era or some shit."

Callum took a solid two minutes to mutter about letter writing not being outdated and how children shouldn't mock their elders. Hunter listened patiently and tried to come up with a more persuasive argument if Callum shot him down.

Then Callum began listing numbers and Hunter recognized the area code for New Brunswick. He dove for the pen on the coffee table, madly scribbling on the back of a magazine.

When Callum was done, Hunter asked, "Wait, what is this?"

"Zach's number, you doofus."

"But *how*? Did you already have it?"

"I texted Barnaby and asked him for it. When he asked why, I assured him it was solely so that you could beg for forgiveness. Now, go forth and grovel, grasshopper."

Hunter huffed. "I don't know why I like you. You're kind of an asshole."

"Please, that's *why* you like me."

He had a point.

ZACH AND BARNABY were tucked in their miniscule, shared office, papers and laptops and coffee cups strewn across every surface. They were arguing about the effectiveness of certain literary devices rather than preparing for the new semester like they were supposed to be doing. Classes would start on Monday and just the thought of standing in front of the class to introduce himself as Dr. Sorenson's TA still gave Zach cold sweats.

Zach was grateful Barnaby had moved on from pep talks about public speaking and the upcoming class. And if previous days were anything to judge by, they'd eventually give up debating the merits of anaphora in favor of heading to a bar or Barnaby's place to watch some hockey.

Basically, Barnaby was the perfect friend.

He was also still beautiful, as well as smart and funny, but any remaining traces of the crush Zach had harbored for Barnaby had blown away like dust in the last couple of weeks.

Ever since Christmas Eve.

Frowning, Zach took a sip of his coffee and told himself to quit dwelling on it. He'd known it was stupid when he'd done it, and he'd been proven one hundred percent correct. He should take the A+ and move on. It had been hot, complete with a truly magnificent orgasm, and now it was in the past. It didn't have to be different than any other hookup.

Except it fucking *was.*

Zach sighed and clenched his jaw shut, refusing to say another word aloud about Hunter. He'd made it all the way to lunch on

Boxing Day before confessing to Barnaby and Travis that he was a complete idiot and that Hunter had pulled a runner.

They didn't even know about all the shit in the past and they'd been suitably sympathetic and outraged on his behalf. Then Travis had invited him over for dinner and to watch a game as consolation for Hunter being such a huge dick.

Again.

Zach sighed. Even prepping for the new semester was better than this ridiculous brooding.

Barnaby was looking at something on his phone, his face scrunched up like he wasn't sure he liked what he saw.

Then he eyed Zach.

"What?" Zach asked.

Barnaby continued to watch him thoughtfully.

"Do I have something on my face?"

Barnaby looked down at his phone and started typing.

Zach ran his tongue over his teeth. "Shit, what do I do if I have something on my face while I'm talking to the class? Like, what if I have a huge booger in my nose? Or, god, something in my teeth? Or what if my fly comes down while I'm lecturing?"

Barnaby dropped his phone into his lap and cast Zach a baleful look. "Has your fly *ever* just magically opened when it shouldn't?"

Zach bit back his first reply, which was, *yes, just this past Christmas Eve, as a matter of fact.*

"No." Zach was aware he sounded sullen about the reliability of his own flies.

"Right. And you can brush your teeth before class, thus eliminating worries about spinach in your teeth and bad breath, and at the same time do a booger check in the mirror," Barnaby said with a firm nod.

Zach's phone buzzed on the desk, but he very deliberately ignored it. He was currently in a battle of wills with his mother, to whom he'd foolishly mentioned seeing Hunter. She was now texting him constantly, convinced Zach was suffering in silent agony or some shit and Zach was refusing to engage except for a single daily text that read: I'M FINE.

Which he was. Because he wasn't thinking about it. It was in the past. He hadn't even brought it up to Barnaby in, like, four whole days, and he was determined to keep the streak alive.

His phone buzzed again. Barnaby looked at it, then arched a brow at Zach. "You going to check that?"

Zach shrugged.

Barnaby tipped forward, the front legs of his chair striking the floor with a thud as his arm slid across the surface to shove Zach's phone sailing into his lap.

Zach caught it, barely.

Barnaby rolled his eyes as he rose to his feet. "*Goalies.*"

"Where are you going?" Zach asked.

"I have the sudden urge to visit Callum," Barnaby announced as he looped his scarf around his neck. "It seems we have much to discuss."

Zach nodded vaguely, his attention captured by a message on his phone.

Unknown Number: I'm sorry. I'm an idiot and I should have left a note.

Something fluttered in Zach's chest, which he chose to believe was due to the burrito he'd had for lunch.

He stared at the message for a long time because there had to be an explanation that made more sense than Hunter fucking Michaelson texting him out of the blue two weeks too late.

Maybe someone hit Zach's car. Or stopped by when he wasn't home?

Zach: Who is this?

Unknown Number: Sorry. This is Hunter. And hopefully the only asshole who has walked out on you.

Zach blinked down at his phone, completely flummoxed. How the fuck was he supposed to reply to that?

He took a second to add Hunter to his contacts, even if he felt like an idiot for doing it. Another message popped up and he switched back to the text app.

Hunter: Because I was a jerk! Not because you shouldn't...or don't...or can't, you know, have people who stay the night or whatever. They just shouldn't be rude assholes like me.

Zach smirked, then tried to frown, annoyed at himself for smiling.

Hunter: Please say something. Tell me to fuck off. Anything. Just please confirm this is the right number and I haven't made an even bigger ass of myself.

Zach: You have the right number.

Zach sent the message grudgingly. The bubbles indicating Hunter was replying immediately popped up, but Zach didn't want to give Hunter another chance to try to be charming. He hadn't earned it.

Zach: So why didn't you?

Hunter: Leave a note?

Or wake me up, you asshole...

Zach: Yes.

The bubbles popped up off and on for a while, and Zach wondered why he was watching it like the most dramatic scene in an Oscar-worthy movie. He'd almost convinced himself to put his phone away and not let himself look for a good long while when Hunter's reply came through.

Hunter: I panicked.

Zach frowned at his phone, extremely dubious. It had taken Hunter two minutes and countless typing sessions to come up with that? Zach couldn't help but wonder what else Hunter had written and discarded.

Also, the fucker really knew how to leave a guy with a lot of questions.

Zach: You mean, like, gay panic?

Hunter: No! Shit I totally deserve that, but NO.

Zach felt something loosen a little in his chest, because he would happily have hit delete and block and walked away if Hunter had said yes. He might have felt some sympathy, but it wasn't his job to hold Hunter Michaelson's hand through any crisis, let alone *that* one.

Hunter: It was my mom, man. She was so fucking pissed at me. You know how she gets. She's scary.

Zach's lips twitched. His recollection of Mrs. Michaelson was that she was very nice, but also something of a steamroller when it came to getting her way.

He shoved aside anything remotely like a fond memory.

Zach: Doesn't really excuse you taking off.

Hunter: I know! I'm so sorry. I swear, I'm not like that. Not anymore. You have no reason to believe me, but my plan was to send you a text and explain. I didn't realize you don't have the same number anymore.

Zach sat with that for a moment because there was a lot to unpack.

Zach: You still had my old number?

Which wasn't the question he should be asking, but for some reason felt really fucking important.

What he should have been asking was how Hunter had his correct number now. Though, in hindsight, Barnaby's sudden desire to see Callum after texting fiendishly and then practically tossing Zach's phone into his lap may have been a clue.

There was a suspicious lack of pending reply bubbles, particularly considering how quick Hunter had been to start his replies up to this point. Zach told himself it didn't matter and started gathering his shit together, jamming his papers and laptop into his bag.

He'd spent enough time on this.

He almost dropped it all to the floor when his phone buzzed.

Hunter: I did. And it turns out your parents' old number doesn't work in the Cayman Islands either.

Zach couldn't decide what was more endearing: the idea Hunter had tried to call his parents to get in touch with him, or that he'd used the correct plural possessive in text.

Both were thawing his attitude toward Hunter and that irked him.

Zach: Well, thanks for reaching out. And for the apology.

Hunter: I really am sorry.

Zach found he could accept that, even if it didn't make any difference. Not really. But it was better than nothing, he supposed.

He tucked his phone in his pocket and grabbed his bag, locking the door behind him as he made his way out of his office toward home. He tried not to think about Hunter the whole walk, but it was hard not to. The guy left an impression, that was for sure.

Zach just wished it wasn't in the shape of a boot print on Zach's ass.

6

Hunter: Can I ask you something?

Zach stared at his phone and wondered if he was coming down with something. Maybe a high fever. Because three beers over the course of one hockey game should not have been enough to make him hallucinate, should it?

What other reason could there be for getting a random out-of-the-blue text from his ex-boyfriend-slash-one-night-stand?

"Zach...*Zach*."

Zach's head snapped up when Barnaby's voice finally registered. He found Barnaby and Travis watching him from their seats at his side.

"You okay?" Travis asked, pitching his voice to be heard over the crowd cheering for the Ice Cats.

"Yeah, I'm fine." He waved his phone vaguely in the air. "Got an unexpected text."

Barnaby smirked. "It wouldn't happen to be from a certain friend in Pittsburgh, would it?"

Zach narrowed his eyes on his friend. "And why would you draw that conclusion?"

"Aside from how you look like someone just slapped your face when anyone so much as mentions him?" Barnaby asked innocently, holding up his plate of nachos like a peace offering. Zach declined. Barnaby took one for himself and studied Zach.

"Are you going to text him back?" Barnaby asked once he'd swallowed.

Zach didn't bother to point out he'd never confirmed who had texted. "I can't see why I should."

"No?" Barnaby stared at Zach as if awaiting answers to questions he'd never actually asked.

Zach sighed. "It's a long story."

"I thought he apologized?" Travis asked, proving he had excellent hearing.

Zach grimaced. "Yeah, he did. But we kind of have this whole history."

Barnaby leaned closer. "Do tell."

Travis looked like he was trying not to laugh at his boyfriend.

Zach pinched his phone between his thumb and finger, turning it end over end against his thigh while he tried to watch the game. Alexei was on fire tonight.

That damn text, though, was like an itch at the back of Zach's brain.

What did Hunter want to ask him? If he was forgiven? If Zach was still angry? About Christmas? About six years ago?

And why the fuck did Zach care?

Maybe it wouldn't hurt to find out.

Or maybe it would be better if they just left well enough alone.

If he could consider being ditched without so much as a note and then a texted apology two weeks later as *well enough*.

Zach stopped playing with his phone and resigned himself to being an idiot.

Zach: Okay.

Hunter: Have I always avoided the top right corner?

Zach snorted and shook his head. Clearly Hunter wasn't dwelling on this shit like he was. He shouldn't feel relieved, but this was definitely an easier issue to address.

Zach: Yes.

Hunter: Really? Even in high school?

Zach: Sorry to burst your bubble, but still yes.

Hunter: Ouch. I don't get it. I do it in practice.

Zach: And never in games. You could have picked the corner over Grandison's shoulder last night in the second period.

It wasn't until he'd hit send that Zach questioned the wisdom of admitting he'd watched Hunter's game. Maybe Hunter would assume Zach had lost his mind and become a New York fan.

Hunter: Fuck.

Zach: You have a mental block.

Hunter: I have A FUCKING MENTAL BLOCK.

Zach could hear the words in Hunter's voice, and it made him want to laugh. Also, an NHL player was asking for Zach's input on hockey. He couldn't pretend that wasn't at least *slightly* cool.

The sound of a throat clearing drew Zach's attention and he turned to find Barnaby and Travis watching him. Travis, because he was a nice person, managed to limit himself to a smirk.

Barnaby, because he was an asshole, was grinning ear-to-ear.

"Shut up," Zach muttered and stuffed his phone back in his pocket.

ZACH: You did it!

Hunter grinned down at his phone, sticking his head into the cubby filled with his rank equipment to hide his face from the rest of the changing room.

They'd just come off the ice after a come-from-behind, third period victory, and he'd barely taken the time to strip off his gross and sweaty top layers before grabbing his phone.

He had fucking *known* Zach would see it, but he hadn't dared hope Zach would text him first. Hunter's masterful plan had been to initiate a conversation by bragging about his accomplishment, but seeing Zach's text...shit, it made his heart skip in his chest.

Hunter: Top right corner!

Zach: Proud of you, buddy.

Hunter flushed, warmed by the kind words even though he was one hundred percent certain Zach was being a patronizing shit and teasing him.

"Yo, Hunter!"

Hunter jumped at the loud yell from right beside him, smashing his head on the shelf and sending his helmet crashing to the floor.

Rubbing his head, he glared at Raf. Luckily, the whole team didn't witness his humiliation, since he'd apparently been smiling at his phone like a simpleton long enough that most of them had already gone into the showers.

"What the fuck, man?" Hunter grumbled at his friend.

Raf grinned winningly. "Sorry, couldn't resist. You trying to get high off the fumes from your pads or something?"

Hunter rolled his eyes. "Yes, that's it. It's a new thing I'm trying out because the trainers said I should stop eating Tide Pods."

Raf cracked up and Hunter shoved his friend toward the showers, promising he'd hurry up so they could grab a bite to eat after.

As soon as Raf was out of sight, Hunter sat on the bench, hunched over his phone.

He didn't know what to write. He didn't know if he *should* write.

He and Zach had a shit ton of baggage, and pretty much all of it was Hunter's fault. It wasn't fair to subject Zach to his company when Zach probably wanted to keep him at arm's length. Hell, it was a miracle Zach was in contact at all.

But this time he'd texted first.

And goddamn it, Hunter wanted more. He had found himself reaching for his phone constantly and had to force himself to put it down. He'd finally caved the other night when he arrived home from practice feeling peevish about the top right corner thing and realized Zach would know if Hunter had always had that problem.

At least, that was the bullshit he used as an excuse for contacting Zach, and he was going to cling to that bullshit for all he was worth.

Hunter: Thanks, man. Has school started again? Last semester, right?

Those magical little dots popped up gratifyingly quickly.

Zach: Yup. First week. Celebrating by grading the first assignment and watching a game.

Something warm and sweet filled Hunter because Zach had volunteered even that much. It felt like an invitation to keep going. To say more.

Hunter: Grading?

Zach: I'm a TA this year. Intro to Lit. 100 freshmen who could not care less.

Hunter: That sounds...fun?

Zach: Ha!

Hunter smiled. He could picture Zach's wry expression.

Hunter: What's the assignment?

Zach: 500 words on whether Rochester is a sympathetic character.

Hunter: uhh...

Hunter would have no fucking idea how to answer that. It would help if he had any clue what book the assignment was about. Maybe.

Zach: The good news is about half the students did some decent work.

Hunter: And the other half?

Zach: I'd say most never bothered to read the book, maybe not even the CliffsNotes. There's also a breathtaking lack of concern for a woman locked in a man's attic and a few who actually dig it. [screaming face emoji]

Hunter blinked down at Zach's text, because he had no fucking idea what Zach was talking about, but ten seconds on Google revealed Jane Eyre sounded more interesting than he'd realized.

Hunter: That all sounds alarming.

Zach: Yes. And worse, this game is going down the f'ing toilet.

Hunter: Who are you watching now?

Zach: Montreal @ Dallas

Hunter: Go Habs!

Zach: Shut your mouth.

Hunter burst out laughing. Some things didn't change.

. . .

ZACH TRIED to play it cool a couple of nights later at Barnaby's house, watching the game and chatting while his brain rioted in a thousand other directions.

It didn't help that Barnaby and Travis kept giving him these careful looks, like he might lose his shit at any moment.

To be fair, it felt a lot more possible than Zach wanted to admit.

He'd seen a lot of players get injured. And not just on TV. He'd witnessed some gnarly shit on the ice right in front of him before. Hell, he'd seen *Hunter* get hurt before.

But not since...

Since nothing. Hunter was still Hunter, and nothing had changed.

Zach spun his phone end over end on his thigh and tried to figure out what the hell was wrong with him. He shouldn't care. Not like this. Not with a tight chest and his stomach roiling with worry.

Not like Hunter getting hurt was on Zach's List of Terrifying Things.

It wasn't even that serious of an injury. Probably. Hunter had been holding the bloodstained towel to his own face and had skated off the ice and walked down the tunnel of his own volition.

It didn't mean anything that the ice crew had to scrape the blood off the ice. There were lots of reasons that happened that weren't particularly serious.

Zach was, like, ninety percent sure both of Hunter's eyes were still in his head where they belonged.

When the commentators announced Hunter would not be returning to the game, Zach's stomach lurched sideways, and he caved.

He started typing ten different messages—*are you okay? do you still have two eyes? hey, buddy, you know that's not how you're supposed to stop the puck, right?*— but in the end, he kept it simple.

Zach: ouch

He didn't expect to hear back for a while since Hunter was probably in the trainer's office. Or hopefully there rather than being taken to the hospital. God, Zach hoped he didn't need a hospital. It was hard to tell if it had been his nose gushing or if his face was cut or what.

Zach really liked that fucking face just the way it was.

And he sort of hated himself for that.

He nearly jumped out of his skin when his phone buzzed in his hand.

Hunter: I'm fine. Just got my face rearranged.

Hunter: [image37]

The selfie made Zach cringe.

"Oh, dear," Barnaby muttered, not even pretending he wasn't peering over Zach's shoulder and reading every word.

"What?" Travis asked. "He okay?"

Zach turned the screen so Travis could see the eye, already swelling and turning black, with a row of fresh stitches bisecting Hunter's right eyebrow.

Travis didn't even wince. "Oh, hey, that's not bad. He should be back on the ice tomorrow."

Zach snorted at Travis's easy dismissal, though he wasn't wrong.

Barnaby rolled his eyes and muttered about hockey players.

Zach: Ow. That'll leave a mark.

Hunter: Cool, right? I think the scar will make me look more mature and menacing.

Zach grinned.

Zach: If it makes you feel better to believe that...

Hunter: It does. It's time for me to move on from the baby face and become a grizzled old veteran.

Zach could imagine what Hunter would look like when he was older, with silver in his hair and crow's feet framing his eyes. Grizzled veterans had never looked so sexy.

Zach despaired that his own imagination would betray him that way.

Zach: I'm pretty sure one scar won't make you grizzled.

Hunter: Just you wait and see.

Hunter: Hey, so while I'm stuck here (trainer's office) and I have you on the phone, I have a question.

Zach: Yes, you still avoid the top right corner.

Hunter: Asshole.

Hunter: I wanted to ask about Mr. Rochester.

Zach stared down at his phone, confused. He'd spent so much of the last week talking about Rochester, it felt like it shouldn't surprise him to have it come up again, except Hunter wasn't one of Dr. Sorenson's students.

Barnaby, who was still making no pretense of doing anything but reading over his shoulder, made a happy sound and nudged Zach.

Zach nudged him back, refusing to be rushed through his what-the-fuck phase for Barnaby's continued entertainment.

Zach: What about him?

Hunter: I guess I wanted to ask if you found him to be a sympathetic character?

Hunter: Because I was surprised when I did.

Hunter: Like, he shouldn't have locked his wife in the attic, obvs.

Hunter: But I feel sorry for him, because in the time and place he lived, there weren't any options. He's kind of trapped.

Hunter: Which, AGAIN, doesn't make locking your wife in the attic okay, but sending her to an insane asylum would have been way worse, especially back then, right? So, he's not, like, totally bad?

Hunter: Then he feels all this love and passion for Jane, but it doesn't matter because society says that's not okay because of Bertha and so he's stuck again.

Zach scrolled through the string of texts three times, trying to make sense of what he was seeing. Not that Hunter was wrong, but Hunter had apparently read *Jane Eyre*, for no reason Zach could determine other than his having talked about it recently.

He didn't know what to think about that. Nor could he possibly explain to anyone why it made him happy, other than that he was obviously an idiot.

Also, Zach *hated* it when people credited shit with a deeper meaning than had ever been intended—a consistent curse in the study of literature—but it was damn hard not to read into Hunter's observations about being trapped by the expectations of society and not feeling as though there were choices.

It seemed like something a gay professional hockey player might know a thing or two about.

Zach bit back a groan, knowing he would spend hours trying to unpack that shit. But unless he wanted to open that can of worms with Hunter—which he didn't—he had to take it at face value and move on.

Zach: Well, you managed something most of the class couldn't.

Hunter: I actually read the book?

Zach grinned, and Barnaby chuckled behind him.

Zach: You got an A on the assignment.

Hunter: Woo! First A since gym class senior year, baby!

Zach laughed helplessly, sending a string of thumbs-up emojis and staring at his phone, eagerly awaiting a response. It took a moment for him to register that the room around him was silent.

He looked up to find the TV on mute and Travis and Barnaby watching him, clearly the better choice for entertainment.

His smile faded. "It doesn't mean anything."

"You sure about that?" Travis asked.

"He's in Pittsburgh. I'm in Moncton. And that's not even close to the biggest issue."

"So?" Barnaby asked.

"So, we're...I don't know. Maybe we can be friends again." Though he had no idea why he should want that. "*Maybe.* But nothing more than that. And even friendship is a long shot."

Travis and Barnaby didn't look convinced, but Travis took mercy and unmuted the TV. Zach, not for the first time in the last week, forced himself to put his phone away and let it go.

7

Z ach was totally freaking out.

Dr. Sorenson wasn't in his office, and when Zach had asked the department admin, he said Dr. Sorenson had gone home sick.

Zach hadn't even known to put this possibility on his List of Terrifying Things.

Dr. Sorenson was never sick. And even when he was, he was totally the kind of asshole who stayed at work, thinking it made him look brave and stoic instead of like Patient Zero of the English Department.

Which meant Dr. Sorenson was *really* sick.

And they had class tomorrow.

It couldn't be healthy for Zach's heart to beat this hard. He staggered toward his office, hoping Barnaby could convince him that just because Dr. Sorenson wasn't in today didn't mean he wouldn't be available to teach tomorrow.

It was bad enough the professor was considering a conference trip in late spring. At least if that happened, Zach would have months to prepare himself.

Though, based on his current state, it might result in months of working himself into a full and proper heart attack.

Said heart plummeted when he discovered the office was empty.

The room wasn't big enough for pacing, but Zach made a valiant effort anyway. He needed to move. He wished he hadn't already been to practice and the gym that morning, because he would have loved to get out on the ice. His head was always clear when he was in the net, his entire focus on guarding the crease and stopping the puck.

He considered going for a run, but his coach would be pissed if he overdid it. They had a big game coming up.

When his phone buzzed, he yanked it from his pocket, hoping it was Barnaby asking if he wanted to meet for coffee or something.

Hunter: Hey! How's it going?

Zach frowned and chewed on his lower lip. He and Hunter had been texting back and forth a bunch since Hunter's injury, and Zach wasn't sure how he felt about it. Well, that was a lie. He felt a zing of excitement every time he saw Hunter's name pop up on his screen. What he didn't know was whether he should, how to stop if he shouldn't, and what was wrong with him in the first place.

Zach: I'm having a meltdown, thanks. How are you?

Zach wasn't sure why he was being so honest, except he'd *really* hoped Barnaby would be here, and now he was alone and desperate for someone, *anyone* to distract him.

Zach's phone rang and he stared in horror at the name HUNTER MICHEALSON flashing on the screen. This was what he got for being a drama queen over text. Hunter's instinct had always been to help people. And to protect Zach.

None of which made answering the phone anything short of stupid, but...

"I'm not sure this is a good idea," Zach said as soon as he put the phone to his ear.

There was a pause before Hunter said, "Okay. I don't blame you, but I want to make sure you're okay. And before we get to that, I should say one thing."

Zach took a deep breath and let it out slowly. "Okay, what?"

"I'm sorry."

"What are you talking about?"

"Christmas. I should have woken you up or left a note. I should have—"

"Didn't we already talk about this?"

"No, we texted, and it's important for me to say it in person, too. Well, over the phone. In my own voice. Whatever, you know what I mean."

Zach smiled, though he did appreciate that Hunter was being earnest. And inadvertently doing an excellent job of distracting Zach from the potential Great Public Vomit Incident of Spring Semester.

"Anyway, I know what I did was wrong. I should have woken you up to say goodbye or left a note. I want you to know, I'm not...I'm not the same person anymore. It wasn't my intent to just..."

"Disappear?"

Hunter's silence felt like a wince.

Zach honestly didn't care. The truth hurt. Also, he was in the middle of a meltdown here, and couldn't deal with a rehash of the past. Not right now.

Hunter sighed. "Right. So, thank you for giving me a chance to say that, and not over text, before you, quite reasonably, hang up on me."

"I'm not going to hang up on you," Zach admitted, though he couldn't say why not.

"Okay, that's good," Hunter said, then cleared his throat. "Uh...so you want to talk about why you're freaking out?"

Zach might have changed his mind about hanging up on Hunter if he hadn't sounded so concerned *and* unsure of himself.

"Dr. Sorenson is sick, and if he doesn't make a miraculous recovery in the next twenty-four hours, I'm going to have to give the lecture to a huge class of freshmen." Zach had started out calmly enough, but by the end he was practically hyperventilating.

"Oh boy," Hunter said. "Still not big on public speaking?"

Of course Hunter remembered and could identify the problem without being told, even after all these years. It was weird to think that in some ways, he still knew Zach.

"Nope." Zach popped the p. "You'd think I'd grow out of it."

"I'm pretty sure that's not how it works."

"Says the guy who does an interview on TV every night," Zach sniped.

"Not every night," Hunter objected. "And one of the reasons I do so many of the post-game and intermission interviews is because some of the guys despise it, so I take their slots."

Zach let his head fall back on his chair and stared up at the water-stained ceiling. "Oh. That's...that's nice of you."

"Eh," Hunter said, dismissing the compliment as had always been his habit. It was both reassuring and scary to think fame and money hadn't changed that. "Does the old picture-them-in-their-underwear trick still not work?"

Zach chuckled at the memory of his senior science presentation. "Sadly, no. And just as well, since I won't have a podium to hide behind in case of an inconvenient boner."

Hunter cackled. "God, you were so worried. I sat in the back of class wondering the whole time if you were blushing from nerves or because you were chubbing up."

"Shut up," Zach grumbled, battling a smile while Hunter laughed. The sound triggered a lot of happy memories and a rush of affection Zach couldn't suppress. "That's a stupid strategy for eighteen-year-old boys, anyway."

"True." Hunter's laughter ended with a long, contented breath. "What if you pictured them all as rookie defensemen?"

"What?" Zach asked, lifting his head off his chair.

"What do you do when a new d-man joins your team?"

"Uh...I don't know. Tell them how we do things because they're all clueless when they first start?" *So clueless.* Like lost baby ducks who hadn't found a mama duck to imprint on or some shit.

"Right. And when they fuck up in the middle of a game?"

"I point it out and tell them we've got this."

"And if they do it right?"

Zach blinked at Barnaby's empty chair. "I whack them on the butt with my stick and say good job?"

"Right," Hunter said, like that was the answer. "Because you're the subject matter expert. The guy who knows what he's talking about. So picture your class as a whole bunch of idiot defensemen and skip the ass-pat in favor of something that won't get you brought up on harassment charges."

Zach's first instinct was to scoff. To blow the whole thing off.

Except, fuck it all, it wasn't a terrible idea. "That could work. I'll think about it."

"Cool," Hunter said, knowing better than to lean on it.

Because he knew Zach.

Zach heard the sound of a fridge door opening, the faint rattling of bottles barely audible through the phone, then the sound of it being shoved closed again. He looked at the clock on the wall. "Time for pre-game pickle juice and peanut butter sandwiches?"

"You bet," Hunter agreed.

Because Zach knew Hunter, too.

HUNTER SWORE he wasn't going to have any expectations or hopes when it came to Zach. He was going to be chill.

So what if a zing of happiness went through him when he saw a new text message come in? That was totally within acceptable limits. He'd found an old friend. Renewed an old friendship.

He was allowed to be giddy.

And yes, maybe they'd restarted this thing with the fuck of the century, but for the last few weeks, they'd just been texting about hockey and school and Hunter's house—which was still in a constant state of construction of some form or another—and Zach's TA job—which sounded perfect for Zach but kept him super busy of late.

Not that Hunter didn't think about Christmas Eve. He did. Like, all the time and twice on nights when his refractory period was almost back to where it had been when he was eighteen. But then, maybe age hadn't been the key factor.

Maybe it was Zach.

But he was *totally* being chill.

He was also racing around the locker room, having half-assed his shower after practice so he could get somewhere quiet and private before Zach got out of class. Dr. Sorenson had the flu and Zach was giving the lecture on personal narratives, including telling the students about their first big writing assignment of the semester.

Well, Hunter hoped he was, because otherwise it meant Zach had passed out in front of the class like he'd promised he would.

He quickly read the texts Zach sent while Hunter had been on the ice. He was worried but also charmed by Zach's blatant attempts to psych himself up while simultaneously pondering the wisdom of wearing a helmet to protect his head when he fell to the floor.

"Hey, Hunter, whatcha doing?"

Hunter jumped, bobbling his phone twice before catching it again. The guys around him cracked up, hooting about his cat-like reflexes and ribbing him about his recent obsession with his phone.

"And what's with the smile?" one of them asked.

"What smile?" Hunter asked, fighting and losing the battle to wipe the smile off his face.

The guys gave him a hard time, but they didn't press, and they didn't slow him down as he threw on his clothes. They were good guys, a few of them bumping his shoulder and giving him knowing looks on their way in and out of the shower room.

He wasn't sure what they thought they knew, but he had a feeling they weren't too far off from the truth.

He shoved aside the instinctive flutter of anxiety. He was determined to follow through on his decision to be himself. With his friends. His team. Himself.

And with Zach.

"You up for lunch?"

Hunter turned to face Raf standing a few feet away, Juri at his shoulder. "I can't today." Without thinking about it, he gestured with his phone.

Raf arched an eyebrow. "You ever going to tell us what's going on there? Because I'm sure we'd all like to know who makes you grin like that."

Hunter laughed and refused to be nervous. *No regrets.* "It's an old friend, and he's about a thousand miles away, sadly. But he's got a big thing today and I've been trying to help. Cheering him on, you know?"

Raf looked curious, and maybe a little confused, like he hadn't been expecting that answer. Or maybe that gender.

Juri looked surprised, but he grinned. "Yeah? Cool. Then maybe tomorrow for lunch?"

"Sure. There's that great place in Edmonton and we should be there in time."

Juri clapped him on the shoulder. "Excellent. Hope everything works out with your friend."

Hunter nodded and pretended he hadn't heard the hesitation before *friend*. "Thanks."

Juri waved him off and turned toward his locker, nudging Raf to follow. Hunter noted the look they sent each other but told himself not to worry. He had a policy against being friends with idiots and bigots, so he had to believe it would be fine.

He hefted his bag and took off for the parking garage.

The drive home took forever, though it was only thirty minutes in the midday traffic to get from their practice facility back into the city. He parked in front of his house because his driveway was full of vans, supplies, and equipment for the guys finishing the basement. His phone rang as he jogged up the front steps, so he veered to the right and sat on the new porch swing.

It was cold out, but the swing was in the sun and sheltered from the wind.

"How'd it go?" he asked without preamble.

"I have more adrenaline running through me right now than after the most intense game ever."

Hunter, god help him, pictured Zach's erect cock and then mentally slapped himself across the face. Maybe that wasn't how Zach reacted to adrenaline anymore, he told himself sternly. They were older now, even if Hunter apparently still had a one-track mind.

"Where are you?" Hunter asked.

"Walking across campus to my office. Why?"

Hunter tried not to preen—and failed miserably—because Zach had called him as soon as he was done with class. "Just curious. Wanted to make sure it's an okay time and place to ask you how it went."

And not at all because I'm a total pervert picturing you striding across campus sporting a semi.

"Yeah, it's a fine time," Zach said, his voice choppy and echoing. Hunter guessed he was running up the stairs to his office. After another few seconds, a door closed, then Hunter heard what sounded like all the air leaking out of Zach.

"You okay?" Hunter asked.

"I'm okay," Zach replied, but it sounded more like a rote answer than a real one.

Hunter changed tactics. "How'd it go? How was it delivering your first lecture, Professor Bloom?" Shit. *Professor Bloom.* Why was that so hot?

Zach's breathing hitched and the hair on Hunter's neck stood on end like he could feel the hot gusts brushing across his skin.

"Well, I did it," Zach said.

"Um...that's good?" Hunter clutched his phone and hoped Zach would give him more to go on.

"I pictured them all as rookies and told myself to act like I was in the net," Zach admitted.

"Yeah?" Hunter smiled so hard his cheeks hurt. "And it worked?"

"It definitely helped. Especially when they started throwing things."

"*What?*"

Zach's laughter filled Hunter with an emotion he didn't dare put a name to. "I'm kidding! It was actually okay. Dr. Sorenson's PowerPoint hasn't changed since I took the class, and Barnaby's notes included that lecture."

"Awesome," Hunter said enthusiastically, "And the assignment? Did that go okay?"

"They had a bunch of questions, some I answered and some I suggested they come to office hours to discuss."

"See? You totally know what you're doing," Hunter said. "I bet you were awesome, Professor Bloom." Hunter couldn't resist saying it again.

Zach cleared his throat. "Thanks." There was a tiny little grunt, followed by a gasp, then silence.

Hunter swung gently, staring out at the park, and told himself he was imagining things. There was nothing to read into the scratch in Zach's voice.

"Are you alone in your office?" Hunter was clearly not fucking chill *in any way* and was going to fuck this up.

There was an unmistakable catch in Zach's breathing. "Yes."

"You still have the same reaction to adrenaline as you did in high school, don't you?"

"Fuck," he groaned. "Not really. Not as much. *Fuck*," he gritted out, "*it's your voice.*"

Hunter went lightheaded from the combination of learning he had that effect on Zach and all his blood rushing to his cock.

"Jesus," he whispered. "Does your office door have a lock?"

"I *can't*—" Zach sounded scandalized, but no less desperate. "You—"

"You should lock the door, Zach," Hunter said in a low voice. He had no idea what the fuck he was doing—dirty phone calls had definitely not been in their repertoire before, and he hadn't tried it since, either.

There was a distinct snick of the lock closing, then the sound of a metal zipper being opened. Zach must have been using the hand holding the phone to do it, which made Hunter wonder what the fuck his other hand was doing.

Hunter could hear each tooth of Zach's fly slip free and a shiver worked down his spine. He shifted on the swing, spreading his legs a little.

Thank god for deep, shaded porches and dead-end streets.

"You, too," Zach murmured. "You have to do this, too."

Hunter closed his eyes and clamped his free hand around the edge of the cushion. "I can't. I'm on my front porch."

"What?" Zach asked, his voice breathy. "Go inside."

Hunter wondered if there was a way Zach could hold his phone so Hunter could hear the slide of Zach's hand over his cock. "My house is full of contractors. I can't walk in with a huge boner and lock myself in the bathroom. God, what if they heard me?"

Zach chuckled, but it sounded thready. "Are they hot?"

Hunter huffed a laugh. "A couple of them are. You should have been here at the start of the season when it was still hot out and the guys working on the roof and siding stripped off their shirts."

"Ungh," Zach gurgled, his breath speeding up. "Fuck you. Why would you make me picture that?"

Because I remember all your buttons.

Hunter clenched the cushion tighter. "Just trying to help. I figure you probably don't have your trusty poster of Callum up in your office."

"*Oh my god*," Zach whispered, but Hunter could hear the laughter in his voice.

"Not spank-bank material anymore?" Hunter wondered.

"Not lately, no," Zach admitted, his voice going a little higher.

Hunter told himself not to read too much into that. "I wish I was there to help you," he murmured. "I could lay you out on your desk—"

"*Fuck*," Zach gasped. "Fuck, *Hunter*. I'm still up against the door. I never made it to my desk."

"God, I'd spread you out and—"

"No time," Zach said, his voice quiet and hoarse. "Fuck, *fuck*, I'm close, I—" His voice cut off with a hitch of breath.

Hunter longed to hear it in person. Every nerve in his body was standing at attention.

When Zach didn't say anything else, Hunter cranked his phone's volume as high as it would go.

"Come on, baby. I want to hear it all," he pleaded.

Zach's only response was a loud whimper, his breath fast and choppy little bursts in Hunter's ear. Hunter's hand ached from where it clenched the cushion by his thigh.

A long, low keening noise came through the phone and arousal tore through Hunter, a gut punch, as he listened to Zach's orgasm from a thousand miles away.

8

Zach tried not to dwell on what he'd done on the phone with Hunter, but it was hard not to think about it, particularly when he was in his office over the next few days. He'd catch himself gazing at the door, remembering the way the hinge had dug into his hip, as a potent flush of arousal and embarrassment warmed his face and made his heart race.

Barnaby actually asked him if he was coming down with something.

And while he was in perfect health, he had the sneaking suspicion he was coming down with a terrible case of *the stupids*.

Since he'd gotten the texted apology from Hunter, Zach had been trying to convince himself that he and Hunter were, at most, rebuilding their friendship. And for a while it had been true. Their conversations resembled the same ones he would have with Barnaby or any of his other friends. School, hockey, television, the devastating toll of being a Raptors fan.

He told himself he was imagining the warmth in Hunter's voice when he asked about Zach's classes. And he hadn't been flirting when he teased Hunter about the most recent publicity pictures released by the team.

Though he'd stand by his assertion that the PR team in Pitts-burgh was perfectly aware of the effect Hunter's ass had on the viewing public and took shameless advantage. Why else would all his pictures be taken at a quarter turn, the swell of his massive butt teasing the viewer?

But Zach hadn't been able to resist calling Hunter the second he was free of the lecture hall and out of earshot of his students. And there had been no mistaking the worry or the warmth in Hunter's voice when he'd answered the phone.

Zach's reaction to it had almost made sense, given his response to adrenaline was sometimes unfortunate. When it happened after an intense game, his goalie gear hid a multitude of sins. Walking across campus in jeans? Well, thank god it was coat season. But no matter when and why it happened, he was a fucking adult, and he could ignore it.

The truth was, though, he hadn't wanted to. Hunter's voice had slid under his skin and dug in. Zach had no more than stepped into his office, dropped his bag and coat on the guest chair, and fallen back against the door before Hunter had known exactly what was going on.

And why was the fact that he was so transparent to Hunter also hot? He'd changed. They both had. But somehow Hunter still *knew*.

The problem was Zach didn't know if it meant anything. He didn't know if he could trust Hunter.

He'd switched back to texting after that call, partly to give himself some space to recover from the blistering intimacy of having jerked off on the phone. It helped that Hunter was on a road trip, and the additional complications of time zone changes, flights, hotels, team buses, and both of them having games and practices meant it was easier to stick to the more flexible mode of communication anyway.

None of this prevented Zach from checking his phone every thirty seconds like a lovesick middle-schooler, but at least he felt marginally more in control. He checked his phone again before he pushed into the Dipsy Doodle Dangle and found Barnaby talking to two men seated at a small table in a cozy back corner. One of the men was so fucking beautiful it was hard not to stare. The other noticed Zach gawping and nodded in his direction, drawing Barnaby's attention.

With a wave of the cup in his hand, Barnaby indicated he'd be right over, so Zach got in line and ordered his coffee, then chose a table in the sunny window. It was midmorning on a weekday, so the tables around him were all empty, which was good because Zach didn't want to risk anyone overhearing him.

Barnaby joined him a minute later, slung his coat on the back of his chair, and settled in. "Sorry about that."

Zach waved it off, then looked out the front window and took a long sip of his coffee. He'd asked Barnaby to meet him, but now he wasn't sure he really wanted to talk about it.

Barnaby lasted maybe two minutes. "Will it be easier if I demand you tell me what's on your mind?"

Zach flashed Barnaby a grateful smile. "Maybe."

Rather than follow through on that, Barnaby only arched a single eyebrow.

Zach folded like a house of cards. "It's Hunter."

"Ah," Barnaby said, not bothering to sound surprised.

"We've been in touch and—"

Barnaby held up a hand. "Define *been in touch*."

"He texted me to apologize." Zach's eyes narrowed on Barnaby's face. "Which you know because you gave Callum my number, didn't you?"

"Guilty," Barnaby said with a shrug. "I thought he owed you an apology. I hope you're not cross with me."

"No, I'm not. I'm really...not," Zach finished weakly.

This time both of Barnaby's eyebrows went up. "So the apology was a good one."

"Uh, yeah. And then we started texting, as you know. And, um, we've spoken on the phone a couple times."

"And that's good, I hope?"

"Yeah, it's been fine," Zach said, meaning it. "Nice, actually. I'm just...confused. Because I don't think it's just a friendship thing."

"Ah," Barnaby said. "And that's bad?"

"With our history? Yeah, I think maybe it is."

Barnaby seemed to consider this, then said, "It would help if I had some idea of what that history is?"

Zach grimaced, because as he got older, he felt more and more foolish about his own role in the entire thing. He studied Barnaby's open, genuinely interested expression and knew he'd find no judgment from his friend, but it was still hard to talk about.

In no small part because he'd never told anyone before.

"We were teammates, here in Moncton."

"I gathered as much," Barnaby said, taking a sip of his coffee, his gaze intent on Zach.

"We weren't friends, really, in school, but we'd played together for years, so we knew each other. Then we started training for our senior year and something changed. First, I thought it was just friendship, kind of out of the blue, but cool. But the way he looked at me made me so nervous, and he was always so *close*. I wasn't sure he realized he was doing it. I knew I was gay, but I didn't think he was, since he'd had a girlfriend up until the summer before. And honestly, at that point, I was certain I was the only gay kid in the entire province, let alone on my hockey team."

Barnaby's smile was bittersweet. "I remember that feeling."

"God, I was terrified it was only a matter of time before Hunter figured me out. He was all over me, and at that age...well, let's just say my ability to control my reactions wasn't great."

Barnaby's smile morphed into a grin. "Like your knob had a mind of its own."

"Exactly!" Zach laughed. "So, one night we're doing homework in my room, and Hunter could have worked anywhere—my desk, the floor, the opposite end of the bed—but he climbs on the bed *right* next to me. He's going off about our history teacher and turns so his legs are practically on top of mine, the whole bed shaking as he rants. I'm clinging to my laptop, using it to cover my reaction, but when I couldn't take it anymore, I put a hand on his knee to at least stop him moving. And, well..."

"The rest is history, as they say?" Barnaby supplied.

"Yeah, pretty much. The next ten months were...amazing, to be honest. We were in this cocoon. And when we were alone together, we were fearless. Honestly, *he* was fearless, and he made it so easy for me to be, too. My parents knew what was going on, and I think his had an idea, but we didn't tell anyone, because everyone knew Hunter was a strong contender to go high in the NHL draft, and neither of us wanted to do anything to fuck that up."

"I can imagine," Barnaby said in a carefully neutral voice.

"It wasn't what you're thinking. He never asked. I didn't want it getting out any more than he did, because then we would have been the center of a shit ton of attention neither of us wanted. He would have been screwed out of a career, if we're being honest, and if you think I'm awkward now, you should have seen me then. Shy doesn't begin to cover it. I would have *hated* it getting out and knowing people were talking about me—*us*—like that."

"I don't think of you as awkward," Barnaby said loyally.

Zach smiled. "Thank you." Then he shuddered, thinking about what would have happened. "I'd still hate to be the subject of that kind of public scrutiny and speculation. It would have been *awful.*"

Barnaby nodded sympathetically.

"Anyway, the long and short of it is..." Zach's voice choked off before he could say the rest, which was stupid. "I thought we could make it work long-term."

"You were in love with him," Barnaby said.

For the first time in a very long time, Zach smiled at the memory. "I was. Utterly and completely. And he loved me, too, I think. He said as much. And I believed him."

Barnaby put his hand over one of Zach's. "And then?"

"And then he got drafted in the first round and left for Denver without me. I thought..." Zach cleared his throat. "I thought I could go with him. I'd put off applying to schools so I could go wherever he ended up. But he went out west for training camp and he never came back. He kissed me goodbye before he left, and I never heard a word from him again."

"Oh no," Barnaby said quietly.

"Yeah, it was awful. At first, I told myself he must be super busy, but more time passed, and I knew. His mom was the one who ended up telling me he wasn't coming home before the start of the season. That's when I knew for sure. I still attempted getting in touch with him, at least to demand an explanation, but it didn't take long before I was too embarrassed to keep trying. I was devastated."

"What did you do?"

"Australia."

"All of it, or just the male half?"

"Ha. You're more right than you know. I spent the first four months of that trip living like a grieving widow and then decided I needed to get him out of my system another way."

"I hope that went well."

Zach sighed happily. "It wasn't terrible."

"Good for you," Barnaby said, squeezing Zach's hand before sitting back. "Though now that I know this, I admire your restraint. It's a wonder you were willing to be in the same room with him. I assume that was the first time you've seen him, when we were at Callum's?"

"God, I had been dreading that moment for so long, and it ended up being both worse and better than I'd thought it would be."

"How so?"

"Well, I don't know if you've noticed, but the man is fucking gorgeous. Like, he was a good-looking boy in school, but now..."

Barnaby smirked. "I did note a certain appeal."

"And that butt..." Zach went on, perhaps a little dreamily.

Barnaby snorted. "Maybe you should get back to telling me how you got from being that sad eighteen-year-old boy to the man who shagged the living daylights out of him a few weeks ago."

Zach cocked his head. "I never said I shagged the daylights out of him."

"Well, call me crazy, but we wouldn't be sitting here having this conversation if the sex had been a disaster."

Zach grinned. "Probably not." He took a sip of coffee and considered Barnaby's question. This was the more difficult part of the story as it made Zach feel foolish. "The truth is, by the time I came back from Australia a year later, I wasn't sad *or* mad anymore. I mean, Hunter had been an asshole. No question. But we'd never talked about what was going to happen. I'd assumed, which was on me. He shouldn't have disappeared, but at some point, I realized I shouldn't have been ready to give up my life and goals for him, carte blanche."

Barnaby nodded. "I made that mistake once, and I was older than you were when I did. I wouldn't suggest it."

"In the end, Hunter probably did me a favor, though I know that's not why he did it."

"And now you're back in touch," Barnaby prompted.

"Right. And while Christmas Eve was an incredibly bad idea, I thought maybe we could get past that and find a way to be friends again."

"But you don't want that," Barnaby said.

"I do! I—"

"No, you want to be with him."

All the breath left Zach's lungs at once. "Fuck. No, I can't want that. How fucking stupid would I have to be to want that?"

Barnaby gave him a long, kind look. "The heart wants what it wants."

"Really? You're going with Emily Dickinson for this?"

"Was she wrong?" Barnaby asked.

Zach sighed. "No, but it doesn't matter, does it? The heart can want whatever, the brain makes sure we don't do stupid shit."

Barnaby smiled knowingly. "That's the theory anyway."

"I can't go down the same road again."

"No, you can't," Barnaby agreed, surprising Zach after the talk about a heart's desire. "In fact, that would be impossible. You're not the same person. Or people. If I may suggest, maybe this time the thing to do is talk to Hunter about it."

Zach would honestly rather poke himself in the eye with one of his skate blades. "We're not there. It was one hookup." And phone sex, but he wasn't going to tell Barnaby about that. "He lives a thousand miles away."

"Be that as it may, there's clearly still something between you two."

"But there shouldn't be. He's never even apologized for what he did. Not really."

"Perhaps that's the conversation you need to have with him first, then. Ideally before you shag the daylights out of him again. Or, might I add, have phone sex in our shared office."

Zach's face went so hot so fast he felt dizzy. "Um...how do you know about that? I would have noticed if you'd been there." Though he had been in a fucking state by the time he'd gotten behind the closed door.

"I should hope so," Barnaby said with a laugh. "And I certainly would have made my presence known before you dropped your trousers," he added, laughing harder.

"Then...*how*?"

Barnaby's eyes sparkled with amusement. "I saw you in the hallway on the phone when you got back from your lecture, and then heard the lock click. And, um..." He cleared his throat. "Smells do tend to linger in those tiny, stuffy offices."

Zach stared at his friend in horror, recalling how Barnaby had come into the office not long after he'd set himself to rights and unlocked the door.

"Jesus Christ," he whispered.

Barnaby smirked. "At least you're not wanking to pictures of my cousin's husband any longer."

Zach put his head down on the table and prayed for death.

HUNTER WAS on the team bus, traveling between the hotel and the arena in Los Angeles, when his phone rang.

He was surprised to see Callum's name pop up on his screen, so he answered, worried something was wrong.

"Callum?"

"Hey, bud. How are you doing?"

"I'm fine," Hunter said, but it sounded like a question. It wasn't that he and Callum didn't call each other, but until recently, it had mostly been when one of them was going to be in the same place as the other and going out for a beer was possible. "Everything okay?"

"Oh, yeah, sure. I was just calling to check in." Callum said it like it wasn't at all weird.

"Uh...really?"

"Well, the last time you called me, you were looking for a certain phone number to make a certain apology, and I have to admit, I'm curious to hear how it went."

"Oh!" Hunter laughed. Callum was just being *nosy*, which was kind of nice, since it was just because Callum cared and not out of some desire for hot gossip.

Not that there was any hot gossip to be had—if Hunter didn't count that whole jerking-off thing he hadn't been able to stop thinking about and was really hoping might happen again when he was somewhere he could join in.

That thought brought him up short, though, as it always did.

"Well?" Callum asked when the silence went on too long.

"I texted him an apology, and it went okay," Hunter offered, keeping it vague as he stood and gathered his things together to get off the bus. "We've texted a bunch since and talked on the phone a couple times."

"That's great," Callum said, sounding more invested than Hunter expected. "So things are going well?"

"Ehhh..." Hunter said. "It's going better than I thought it would, anyway. Maybe better than I deserve."

"Want to explain that to me?"

Hunter veered off from the line of players walking to the arena. It was nice to be outside without freezing his balls off, and he didn't want to have this conversation in front of an audience. He waved his friends and the coaching staff on, promising he'd be along in a minute.

He found a quiet spot not far from the door and told Callum the truth. "I was a dick back when we were kids. And as much as I'd like to pretend I wasn't and that the whole thing has gone away, it hasn't."

"You still feel guilty," Callum ventured.

"I still *am* guilty."

"What did you do?" Callum asked, and Hunter was flattered by his clear bewilderment, like it was hard for him to believe Hunter could have been a total asshole.

"I got into the NHL and pretended Zach didn't exist." Because he *had* been a total asshole.

"*Ouch.*"

"Yeah. I was in a panic," Hunter admitted. "I thought I'd be kicked out, that I'd never make the team, that...shit, I can't even remember what I was thinking."

"You know I understand."

Hunter felt another rush of gratitude for Callum's friendship. "I do remember being terrified someone would discover I had a boyfriend."

"Is that what he was?"

Hunter sighed. "Yeah. He was the real deal. I loved him."

There was a pause. "And now?"

Now the longing was so strong, it took his breath away sometimes. "I don't know what we are. Friends, maybe? Sometimes I think it's more, but it can't be."

"Why not?"

"We were in love, and I *ruined* it. Absolutely burned it to the ground. Worse, I sacrificed him for my career, like some asshole in a Hallmark movie. I knew it wasn't the right thing to do at the time and hindsight has only made it clearer what an idiot I was. And that was before I saw him again."

"Oh boy," Callum murmured.

"He should hate me."

"But he doesn't. He still talks to you in spite of your past," Callum observed.

"Maybe because I force the issue," Hunter said, confessing something he'd been worried about since the first text.

"Do you? He never calls or texts you first?"

"He does. Sometimes." Hunter could detail every instance, truth be told.

"You know, even us old fogies know there's that fancy block function on them there new-fangled phones," Callum said, sounding like a shaky-voiced octogenarian.

Hunter laughed. "Shut up."

"I'm just saying, I don't think you *forced* him to be your friend again."

Hunter made a noncommittal sound.

"Do you want to be with him?"

Hunter took a shaky breath. "I'm trying not to think about it, to be honest, because it doesn't seem possible."

"What would it take? To make it possible?"

Hunter *had* thought about this. A lot. "An apology from me, as a start."

"What else?"

Because they both knew it wasn't so simple.

"I can't be that guy anymore," Hunter said.

"What guy?"

"The one who was so afraid that he put himself before everyone else. The one who hurt Zach. Who didn't just end it but did it cruelly."

Callum let out a long sigh. "Okay, listen to me, Hunter Michaelson. You fucked up. You handled things poorly and you know it."

"So far this pep talk leaves a lot to be desired."

Callum ignored him. "But you're not a cruel person. You're not an asshole. You're not undeserving of love from Zach or anyone else. And you're not the same person you were six years ago."

"How do you know?" Hunter asked, embarrassed by the plea in his voice.

"Because I knew you then and you were just a kid. And while that doesn't excuse your behavior, it goes pretty far toward explaining it. Could you have had this conversation back then?"

"Never."

"Right. You didn't even have the tools back then. Who does at eighteen? You've grown up."

"Are you sure?"

"Look, you came to see me at Christmas because you don't want to live with regrets. You don't want to hide from the people you care about. It takes a certain amount of maturity to take a look at yourself and your life and acknowledge change is needed. Hell, I didn't get there until I was almost a decade older than you are."

Hunter didn't know what to say.

"The kicker is that now comes the hard part," Callum added.

"What do you mean?"

"Now you have to *do* it. Be the kind, thoughtful adult-Hunter you want to be."

"I need to apologize," Hunter stated, more certain than ever. It wasn't just the first step; it was an absolute prerequisite for anything else. Not just as a means to build a friendship—or more—with Zach, but because it was the right thing to do. *That* was who he wanted to be.

"Right. And while you work on that, do me a favor?" Callum asked.

"What's that?"

"Try to forgive yourself, too."

Hunter sighed and wished, desperately, that Callum and he still lived in the same city during the season so Hunter could hug him. "Yeah, okay."

9

Hunter gazed at the Los Angeles hills, still blanketed in lights at almost midnight. They'd just gotten back to the hotel after a tough game and the balcony off his room had looked like the perfect spot to clear his mind.

He had a hard time settling after losses, even when he was home. Even when he didn't have something on his mind, demanding his attention. And while the fresh air and beautiful view helped, he couldn't quiet his head.

He considered going down to the hotel gym and running his ass off, but while his brain was fired up, his body was sore and tired.

He'd be wiser to jerk off for that hit of dopamine, except he was anxious and he didn't think his dick would cooperate. What he definitely didn't need was to fail at masturbating.

Which left him staring into the night like the emo hero of some flick the critics at Sundance would love.

Snorting at his own wandering thoughts, he clutched his phone in his hand and sighed. He knew what would fix him better than anything and he'd just have to hope it wouldn't be the last conversation he and Zach ever had. And even if it was, he'd feel better—*eventually*—for having done it. It was long, long overdue.

Hunter hit dial, realizing too late that if it was midnight in LA, it was ass o'clock in Moncton.

"Hey," Zach answered, his voice scratchy with sleep. "Everything okay?"

Hunter focused on the worry in Zach's voice, hoping like hell it meant he cared at least a little.

"Yeah, everything's good. I'm sorry for calling so late. I just...I wanted to talk to you about something."

"Okay," Zach said warily.

Hunter stepped back into his room and closed the door, then perched on the end of his bed and took the plunge. "I'm sorry I disappeared. When we were kids. I'm sorry I left and never got in touch. That I ignored you. That was"—Hunter stopped, throat tight—"wrong. *I* was wrong."

His hastily delivered out-of-the-blue apology was met with silence, and Hunter died a little inside with each second that passed.

"Why'd you do it?" Zach asked in a quiet voice.

Hunter considered saying he'd been young. Foolish. Distracted. Careless. But that wasn't the whole truth. The real reason.

"I was scared."

Zach went silent again and Hunter made himself breathe. He wanted to demand a response, but when an apology was six years late, he could damn well wait as long as Zach needed.

"Of what?" Zach asked.

"God," Hunter said on a sigh. "Everything. Of making the team. Of *not* making the team. Of being gay. Of being caught. Of dragging us both into the spotlight, you hating me, and me losing my spot on the team. Of being not cool enough for the rest of the guys on the team. Or being too young. Too stupid. Of being—"

"Hunter."

Hunter closed his eyes. "I'm sorry," he said quietly. "That doesn't matter. None of that matters."

"What do you mean?"

"I mean, it makes no difference what I was afraid of. None of that excuses what I did to you. You were scared, too, and you didn't—" He swallowed past the lump in his throat and forced out the words that hurt to think, let alone say. "I threw us away. Worse, I did it cruelly and in a way that hurt you and probably made you believe I didn't care. That I didn't love you. And I did."

Hunter couldn't remember ever feeling more raw, more exposed, than he did in that moment. The protracted silence that met his brutally honest admission was torture and it still felt like the least he deserved. If Zach hung up and never contacted Hunter again, he'd understand. The only thing that was hard to understand was why Zach had let Hunter back into his life at all.

"Okay."

Hunter blinked at his reflection in the dark TV screen.

"Okay?"

"I mean, it *wasn't* okay," Zach clarified. "But thank you for apologizing. I can, looking back, imagine how scared you must have been."

"Thanks," Hunter said, humbled by Zach's generosity.

"And now?" Zach asked.

"I'm still sorry?" Hunter offered, not sure what Zach was asking.

Zach laughed quietly. "No. I mean, are you still scared of that stuff?"

Oh.

Hunter's first instinct was to say no. His second, fortunately, was to be honest.

"Some of it, I guess. The whole *dragged into the spotlight* thing still doesn't hold a lot of appeal for me."

Zach hummed. "I can understand that."

"But the other stuff?" Hunter shrugged, even though Zach couldn't see him. "I'm not worried about losing my spot. Or the guys liking me."

"Because you've proven yourself?"

"No. Well, yes, I hope so, but I don't mean like that. I mean, like, if I were to, for example..." Hunter gulped. "Have a boyfriend. I wouldn't be worried about that stuff."

There was a rustling sound, like maybe Zach was sitting up. "Are you sure? Because there are still a lot of people, especially in hockey—"

"No, I know. There will be guys who won't be okay with it. But if those guys found out? Fuck them. And my friends would be cool."

"Are you sure?"

"Um...*yeah*. I'm pretty sure my friends suspect already about me. And, uh...you. They've been giving me a hard time for smiling at my phone a lot."

"Oh," Zach said, and Hunter thought it sounded happy. He *hoped* that was a happy *oh*. "That's..."

"Not meant to pressure you," Hunter finished quickly. "I just... uh...wanted you to know."

"Thanks," Zach said.

Hunter wasn't sure what Zach was thanking him for, but it felt like a good thing. A really good thing.

ZACH HAD a lot on his mind in the weeks following his late-night conversation with Hunter. He'd needed to hear that apology. He'd needed to know why Hunter had done what he had all those years ago and that he regretted it.

It left Zach thinking a lot about forgiveness. He could imagine the fear Hunter had experienced and empathize, but that alone wouldn't have been enough for Zach to not only accept the apology but move on. The apology had been necessary, but it wouldn't have held any weight if he hadn't seen and heard and felt how Hunter had changed in the intervening years. That was how Zach knew Hunter meant it and understood what he'd done and felt genuine remorse.

So Zach could move on now. The tricky part was figuring out where he was moving on to, both literally and figuratively.

Hunter had definitely thrown him a curveball when he'd dropped the B-word into the conversation. *Boyfriend*. Was that what Hunter wanted? Zach hadn't asked, and he wasn't *going* to ask because they'd barely seen each other. Yes, they'd spent hours on the phone and sent millions of text messages back and forth over the past month. And yes, the flirting sometimes got intense. And yes, it was hot.

But it wasn't enough to know what they wanted from each other yet.

Except for how Zach *did* know.

With a sigh, he put his head down on his crappy office desk and told himself to stop worrying about shit he couldn't do anything about and start focusing on the shit he had to do. It was late and he'd purposely stayed in his office to get some work done. If he were at home, he would've been too tempted to turn on the TV. He'd always loved watching hockey, but now he did it knowing all the funny, sad, poignant, infuriating, hysterical, and bewildering stories Hunter had told him about guys all over the league and it was even better. Irresistibly so.

If Hunter had been playing, Zach would have watched, work be damned, but Hunter was flying home from the West Coast tonight. Zach's phone had been quiet for the last few hours and his schoolwork was done, so he'd taken the opportunity to get caught up on his current work projects. He'd taken the job as a contract copy editor a few years back at the encouragement of one of his creative writing professors, who'd seen Zach's markup of a classmate's paper.

It ended up being an ideal way to support himself through the remaining years of school. He was quick and good with details, so his customers loved him, and he could clear enough work to pay the bills. And since he mostly worked on shorter pieces like scientific publications and magazine articles, he could easily adjust how much work he accepted during busier times, like finals.

He could also do it from anywhere in the world with an internet connection, which meant he didn't have to worry about losing this income when he went to grad school.

But only if he could focus long enough to do his damn job. With a determined grunt, he got down to business, refusing to check the clock until the mind-numbingly boring article on the health-improving effects of a certain species of mushroom was complete. He fired it off to his customer, then packed up and walked home, letting the sting of the cold air clear his head.

When he got there, he found a package waiting for him in the little foyer just inside the door from the street. He grabbed his mail, along with the carefully taped and sealed tube, his heart skipping when he saw it was shipped from Pittsburgh.

He darted up the stairs, leafing through the rest of his mail while trying to calculate if Hunter's plane had landed yet. When he came across the letter from Carnegie Mellon University he stuttered to a stop in the middle of his kitchen.

His bag and coat hit the floor with a thump and he tore into the envelope, nearly ripping the letter as he yanked it free. The words swam in front of his eyes before they finally took shape and made sense.

Holy shitballs, I'm in.

Zach broke into a wild dance around his kitchen involving a lot of pumping fists and leg kicks. When he was done, he read the letter again, this time going past the words "you've been accepted" and noting the request that he visit this spring to meet with potential advisors and discuss financial options for his first year with the program, should he choose to attend.

He fell into a chair, his heart pounding as he absorbed the fact that he needed to go to Pittsburgh.

Fucking *Pittsburgh,* of all places.

Just for a visit, but...

He suddenly couldn't remember if Carnegie Mellon had always been his first choice. He thought so, but a thread of fear worked its way into his brain. Was he letting himself be drawn in the wrong direction for the wrong reasons?

He tried to settle his whirling thoughts into something beyond *Pittsburgh, Pittsburgh, Pittsburgh* but it was pointless. With shaking hands, he dug his phone from his pocket. His first instinct was to call Hunter, but he shoved that aside.

Zach: What is my first-choice grad program?

Barnaby: You're asking me?

Zach: Please. Just answer the question.

Barnaby: Carnegie Mellon.

Zach took a deep breath and let it out slowly.

Barnaby: Are you okay?

Zach assured Barnaby he was fine. He didn't tell him about the letter. Zach needed time to think before he got any input, particularly from anyone who knew what—or rather, *who*—was in Pittsburgh. But he did believe Barnaby. And himself.

CMU *had* been the dream all along.

And now...well, fortunately, he didn't have to make any decisions right away. For starters, he was still waiting to hear from the two other schools and until he did, he didn't know what his options truly were. Being accepted was one thing, but there was still a lot to learn, particularly when it came to the costs of the programs and what kind of financial assistance, if any, was being offered. Zach was hoping to do this without ending up buried under a mountain of debt.

Turning to the mess he'd made on his way into the house, he hung his coat and bag on the back of his chair and gathered the rest of the mail from where he'd scattered it across the counter. He reached for the tube from Pittsburgh. He'd assumed it was from Hunter, but maybe CMU had sent him something.

He tore into the package.

Then he called Hunter.

"You did *not* send me a poster of yourself," he said as soon as Hunter answered, trying to sound indignant.

Hunter cracked up. And god help him, Zach did, too.

"I thought you might need a replacement for your poster of Callum," Hunter explained, clearly delighted with himself. "I noticed it was missing at your new place."

"I cannot believe you," Zach said, still laughing. "You fucking *signed it*. You're such a dick."

"I am." Hunter sounded proud. "If you hang it up," he added, his voice dropping to a low and sexy rumble, "I can tell you a bedtime story."

Zach shivered. He could only fucking imagine what that would be like. So could his dick, damn it. They weren't really doing this phone sex thing again, were they? Zach had been viewing his previous indiscretion in his office as a fluke.

If it was possible to have a masturbatory fluke.

"You're ridiculous," Zach said, his voice uneven.

"Yeah? But you're thinking about it, aren't you?"

Fuck, was he ever. "Aren't you at the airport or something?"

"Nope. Just got home a few minutes ago and now I'm collapsed on my couch. So...what are you wearing?"

"Fuck off," Zach said. "What are *you* wearing?"

"My charcoal suit," Hunter answered, voice smug.

Goddamn it. He'd told Hunter just last week that his ass looked obscene in that suit.

"I'll be keeping this one in frequent rotation," Hunter promised.

Zach stood in his kitchen, looking between his bedroom door and his new poster.

Oh, fuck it.

"I can't believe I'm doing this," he muttered as he stomped into his bedroom.

"What?" Hunter asked.

Zach yanked four pushpins from the corkboard over his desk. "I'm putting up the goddamn poster, okay?"

Zach listened to Hunter's laughter as he kicked off his shoes, climbed onto his bed, and pinched the phone between his ear and shoulder.

"Where are you going to hang it? On the ceiling above your pillow?" Hunter asked, trying to make his voice sound sexy but failing miserably because he couldn't stop snickering.

"Fuck you," Zach mumbled around the pins he held between his lips while he shoved the first into the corner of the poster. After three pins, he was able to clarify. "It's on the wall beside the bed, you dick. I can't believe I'm doing this."

"Yes, you can," Hunter said.

"You're wearing all your equipment, for Christ's sake."

"Should I have sent you a big picture of me in this suit?"

"I would already be naked," Zach admitted, enjoying the choking sounds coming from the other end of the call.

Turning the tables was fun.

"You going to join me this time?" Zach asked.

He didn't have Hunter's ability to drop his voice, but it didn't sound like he needed it, anyway.

"*Fuck,*" Hunter moaned.

Zach was on his back on the bed with his jeans around his thighs in seconds. He couldn't fucking believe they were doing this, but Hunter was already panting, and Zach's body was primed just hearing it.

He scrambled with one hand in the bedside drawer. The lube was shockingly cold when he wrapped his hand around his shaft, but it wasn't even close to enough to slow his dick from getting fully hard.

"Tell me," he demanded, unable to listen to Hunter gasp one more fucking time and not *know*.

"What?" Hunter asked.

"Are you close? Are you going fast and tight, or nice and slow?" Hunter's whimper went right down Zach's spine. "Tell me. *Please.*"

"Fast and tight," Hunter gasped out. "Fuck. Way *too* fast. This isn't going to take long. I'm—"

Hunter's moan went in Zach's ear and straight to his cock.

Zach's own hand sped up. His ass clenched, his hips punching up into his fist as he closed his eyes and imagined Hunter sprawled on his couch, his gorgeous suit in disarray as he jerked his perfectly perfect cock.

"Come on, Hunter," Zach coaxed, breathless. "I want to hear you."

Fuck, how could it feel so good just to listen to Hunter's unsteady breaths?

At some point he'd give Hunter shit that Zach had been expected to converse the last time they'd done this, and now that the tables were turned, Hunter could do little more than make obscene noises.

Right now, those noises were really working for Zach. Hell, they were driving him out of his goddamn mind.

His eyes lifted to Hunter's image on the wall as Hunter cried out his name. It should have been ridiculous, but damned if Zach wasn't coming his brains out two seconds later.

Jesus Christ.

Zach lay stunned, listening to Hunter's harsh breaths, out of sync with his own.

"God, I miss you," Hunter said, his voice wrecked.

Zach's breath hitched, his heart stumbling in his chest. "You do?"

"Yeah," Hunter said, like it was obvious.

And Zach had a lot of thoughts about that, things he wanted to say in return but was afraid to, things he could say but didn't begin to cover what he was feeling.

What came out of his mouth was, "I'm coming to Pittsburgh."

Hunter's breathing cut off all together. "What?"

"I have to meet with people at Carnegie Mellon, and I thought maybe we could—"

"Yes. Whatever the rest of that sentence is, my answer is yes. Unless you were going to say you thought we could avoid each other, then it's no. But yes to seeing each other. Yes to spending some time together. Shit, when are you here? Fuck, I hope I'm home. I might have games somewhere. But you could stay here. At my place. If you wanted. Even if I'm not here, you're welcome."

Wow. "Okay, that's"— where did he even start? —"really nice of you."

Hunter scoffed. "Please, this is totally self-serving. I'll take whatever time you can give me. I'm sure you'll have a bunch of stuff you have to do while you're here."

Zach didn't know what he'd expected, but Hunter wasn't putting up any pretenses. He was just laying it out there, and while it was a little scary, Zach appreciated it.

"I'll have some things I have to do, but I can choose the dates, so I could ask about..." Zach squinted at the schedule he'd tacked up above his desk, able to make out enough from the color coding to determine when Hunter had home games. "What about two weeks from now? You're home to play Minnesota and San Jose."

Hunter agreed enthusiastically and they went back and forth on some alternate dates so they had a couple of options. Zach promised to let Hunter know when he heard back from CMU since their input would decide which was the best choice.

Hunter sounded excited the whole time they made their plans and Zach found himself grinning like a simpleton at the ceiling above his bed.

Whatever was happening between him and Hunter, it felt good. And he definitely wasn't alone in wanting it. Whatever *it* was.

And would it make any difference if Zach didn't end up in Pittsburgh in the end?

Because no matter how much he wanted to be with Hunter, he couldn't pick Pittsburgh just for that. For him.

10

———

Zach woke up nervous the day of his trip to Pittsburgh. Fortunately, there was no greater distraction than a flight to Toronto, wrestling his way through Pearson International Hellport, then a short hop to Pittsburgh. He landed on time, which meant Hunter was still at practice. The plan was for Zach to get the bus into the city, then either walk or take a taxi to Hunter's place. There was a chance he'd get there a few minutes before Hunter, but he'd promised it wouldn't kill him to wait on the front porch.

He was trying to watch where he was going while checking his phone to see if he had any messages from Hunter when he caught sight of a man holding a whiteboard with BLOOM written on it. He considered ignoring it since Zach wasn't the only Bloom in the world.

Then the driver looked at him and said, "Zach?"

Zach blinked at the uniformed livery driver. He was in his fifties with some salt in the pepper of his dark brown hair and what Zach's father would have called a dad bod. "Uh, yeah?"

"Hunter asked me to come get you," the man said as he tucked the whiteboard under his arm and plucked Zach's duffle from his hand. "I'm Mark."

"Oh, ah, wow. Thank you," Zach said. He thrust out his hand. "I'm Zach."

Mark smiled and shuffled Zach's bag so he could shake hands. "I know. Hunter said I would be a surprise and sent me your picture in case you didn't see my sign or didn't think it was for you."

"Guilty," Zach said with a helpless shrug.

Mark grinned. "Guess Hunter knows you, then."

Zach had no idea what to say. It was hard to know what to *think* when he was staring up at a three-story image of Hunter and two of his teammates welcoming all travelers to Pittsburgh.

Fuck, how had Zach gotten all the way here without realizing what it meant that Hunter was famous? He'd known Hunter was recognizable to a lot of hockey fans, but that was different than seeing *this*.

"Cool, right?" Mark said with a nod toward the team's thirty-foot-tall welcome sign.

"Yeah. Right." Zach tried not to gulp too obviously. His general nerves about seeing Hunter were replaced with the very specific worry that this might be a huge mistake.

The ride into the city was quick at this time of day and also an education in how much the coal mining industry still impacted the area. The city itself was beautiful, and so much bigger than Moncton, but still small compared to some of the places Zach had visited. He liked that it had more to offer than home but wasn't as anonymous as New York or even Boston would be.

They turned off one of the broad city avenues into a quiet residential area, then turned onto an even quieter street that circled a narrow park with modest family houses lining both sides. Each had a deep front porch, with small driveways tucked beside them. They swung around the end of the square to stop in front of the last house, tucked into a corner between its neighbor and what looked like a large, wooded area.

"This is it," Mark said, parking along the end of the street so he wouldn't block the driveway.

Zach couldn't remember what he'd been expecting, but it hadn't been this. He'd never thought to ask for more than an address and hadn't looked it up. Hunter had talked about owning a house and doing work on it, but still. This was...

...a *home*.

Not just a single-family house, but one with curtains in the windows and striped cushions on the porch swing that matched the trim. The bricks were unpainted, the red warm and bright against the grays and whites of week-old snow.

"You want me to wait here with you?" Mark asked. "Hunter said he might be a few minutes late."

"How do you know Hunter?" Zach asked, noticing how fond Mark sounded every time he said Hunter's name.

"My company does a lot of work for the team," Mark said with an easy shrug. "You get to know some of the guys. Hunter's a good kid. One of the ones who actually pays attention to the people around him, you know what I mean?"

Something settled in Zach. "I do." Hunter was famous, but somehow, he was also still Hunter.

"And there he is," Mark announced as a sleek black car zipped past them and into the driveway. Hunter barely waited for the car to come to a complete stop before jumping out.

Mark climbed from the front seat and opened Zach's door, which felt super weird but Zach couldn't worry about it. His eyes were glued to Hunter and his huge smile as he jogged toward them.

For a moment, right before Hunter hugged him, Zach was sure he was about to be kissed. Heart racing, it took him a second to collect himself and return Hunter's hold. When he did, Hunter squeezed even tighter.

Zach wasn't a big fan of public displays of affection, but he couldn't make himself let go. Hunter turned his head, burying his nose in Zach's scarf, and hummed quietly. Zach curled his hand over the nape of Hunter's neck and took a deep breath. He felt oddly relieved, like he'd just come home from a long trip.

Mark cleared his throat and they stepped apart. The driver's eyes darted between them, his smile wide and knowing.

Geez, Hunter might as well have kissed him. Not that Zach cared, but he was curious what Hunter's reaction to Mark's perceptiveness would be.

"I'll take that," Hunter said cheerfully, reaching for Zach's bag. "Thanks, Mark. You need anything before you head out?"

"Nope. I'm good," Mark said. "I'll see you tomorrow night," he added to Zach as he climbed into the car with a final wave.

"Why will I see Mark tomorrow night?" Zach asked as the man drove away.

"He's going to bring you to the game and then you can come home with me."

Zach felt both spoiled and guilty. "I can take a bus."

Hunter shrugged. "You can, but I'd feel better if you had a ride. If you want, I can have Mark take me to the arena and you can drive my car."

Zach laughed and eyed the very fancy vehicle in question. "A Tesla, huh?"

"I'm very green," Hunter said in a snotty voice as he turned toward the house.

Zach followed, laughing, because the truth was Hunter *did* care about shit like that and they both knew it.

What was worse—or better?—was that Zach really loved that about him.

He followed Hunter up the wide front porch steps and took in the warm, inviting house beyond the picture window and the little tables to either side of the porch swing, just waiting for company and drinks on a warm night. It was all a little surreal, but it still wasn't enough to distract Zach completely from Hunter's perfect ass in the slightly too tight sweatpants he'd worn home from practice.

Zach wondered if Hunter had chosen them on purpose until Hunter stooped to open his front door, bending at the waist and sticking his ass out to get the key in the lock.

Yeah, he'd definitely worn those on purpose.

Feeling brave and very much invited, Zach slid closer, blocking the view from the neighbors, and clamped his hand around one delicious ass cheek.

Hunter gasped and planted a hand on the door.

Zach dug his fingers in. "I guess I'm just lucky you're not wearing the charcoal suit."

Hunter's low chuckle vibrated across Zach's skin. "I'm saving that for tomorrow."

Zach squeezed harder. "You're a tease."

"It's not teasing if I have every intention of following through."

Zach's mouth went dry. "Get the fucking door open. *Please.*"

Hunter fumbled with the key, finally managing to unlock the damn door and almost falling inside. Zach followed him, laughing, his hand still attached to Hunter's ass.

The door had barely closed when Zach was pinned to it, his arms full of Hunter Michaelson.

"Tell me this is okay," Hunter gasped, lifting onto his toes to align their bodies. "Tell me you want this."

"God, Hunter," Zach groaned, sliding his fingers into Hunter's short blond hair, still damp from his post-practice shower. He crushed Hunter's lips beneath his own in a wet, open-mouthed kiss that skipped right over polite greeting and landed firmly on *take your fucking clothes off right now.*

Hunter understood, his hands everywhere at once, yanking off his coat and shoving at Zach's while Zach was incapable of doing more than clinging to Hunter's ass and keeping their bodies as close as possible.

When Zach was finally forced to let go, he shucked his top layers and watched Hunter do the same, then he pushed Hunter against the wall and caught his mouth in another kiss.

Hunter's groan went straight to Zach's dick.

So did Hunter's hands. Zach ground against the warm palm cupping him through his jeans and gasped against Hunter's lips.

"God, I want to fuck you."

Hunter nodded, vigorously, which forced an end to their kiss. Zach stared down at wide, glazed eyes and suddenly missed Hunter for all the years they'd been apart. He'd tried to hate Hunter for some of them, forget him for the rest, but now, here, he could lament the time lost, even if it had probably been for the best.

"Please, Zach," Hunter whispered.

"Yes," Zach agreed, kissing Hunter again. "Where? We need—"

Hunter arched off the wall, his strength sending a thrill down Zach's spine even as he tried to keep his feet under him and his grip on Hunter. They staggered, shoulders bouncing off walls as Hunter dragged Zach across the entryway while also trying to kiss him. It didn't work and for the second time in five minutes, they almost fell through a door, this time into the little half bath off the front hall.

Zach took in the lavender walls and the delicate pedestal sink and tried to make sense of it. Hunter's house was warm and real and nothing whatsoever like the rich-dude bachelor pad Zach had been expecting—without judgment. Hell, Zach's place was about a thousand times more bachelor pad-like than this.

Then Hunter slapped a bottle of lube against Zach's palm, and all thoughts about tastefully matching and yet somehow masculine pewter and purple hand towels fled his mind.

"You keep lube in the guest bathroom?" Zach asked.

Hunter paused in the process of shoving his sweatpants and boxer briefs over his hips. Zach's eyes latched onto the taut lines of Hunter's abdomen and the V-shaped cut of muscles as Hunter's cock sprang free.

Still perfect.

"Where else would I keep it?" Hunter asked.

Zach had to force his brain to think about something other than getting his mouth around Hunter's dick. Then he laughed because that was both a ridiculous question and one for which Zach had no good answer.

"Fair enough," he admitted, as he wrapped his hand around Hunter's cock.

All the air left Hunter's lungs in a shaky rush. His hands clenched the edges of the sink. Zach hoped the thing was sturdier than it looked.

"Turn around."

Hunter's eyes flared before he turned his back and gripped the sink again.

Zach sank to his knees, dropping the lube onto the floor nearby and then wrestling with his jeans, ripping them open and shoving them down enough to get his dick unbent. He looked up to find himself faced with a particularly gorgeous hockey butt. Jesus, Hunter's ass was magnificent.

Zach leaned in and rubbed his face over the swell of Hunter's cheeks, dotting kisses over the soft skin. He gripped the firm globes and pried them apart, his tongue darting out to lick Hunter's hole.

Hunter let out a loud, startled cry. "No!"

Zach jerked back and Hunter slumped over the sink.

Zach's confusion turned to genuine alarm. "Hunter?"

Hunter spun to face him, his face flushed almost crimson. He looked freaked out. Zach started to climb to his feet, but Hunter stopped him by kneeling on the floor between Zach's thighs.

"No one..." Hunter licked his lips and swallowed hard. "No one has ever done that before. To me."

"Okay," Zach said, still uncertain how to interpret Hunter's reaction. "We don't have to."

"God, I hope we do, but I swear to fucking god, I'll come instantly. I want your cock in me, Zach. I've been *dreaming* about you fucking me. I don't want to blow it by...well, blowing it."

Zach huffed a laugh, a little dizzy from Hunter's breathtaking honesty. "Okay," he choked out, voice hoarse. He curled his hand around Hunter's cock, still as hard as a pike. "But at some point— today, tomorrow—I'm going to eat you out until you're screaming for more."

Hunter let out a little whimper. "Fuck, you fight dirty."

Zach got a little lost in Hunter's warm hazel gaze. He rubbed a bead of pre-come over the smooth cap of Hunter's cock and watched the flush of arousal spread from his cheeks down his neck. Zach reached for the lube, but Hunter shook his head and poured some over his own fingers, his eyes never leaving Zach's as he stretched that arm behind himself.

His wide, earnest gaze heated, his eyelids dropping to half-mast. Zach's heart fluttered, trapped and frantic in his chest as Hunter prepped himself.

Jesus, that was hot.

Hunter pushed Zach with his free hand, tipping him backward until Zach's bare ass hit the cool floor tiles and his back rested against the pretty lavender wall. He shucked his jeans, fished the condom out of his wallet, and rolled it on, touching himself as little as possible in the process. He couldn't take his eyes off Hunter as he crawled over Zach, shedding sneakers and sweatpants until he hovered on his knees, completely naked.

Zach stared up at a man he'd known for years but had never seen before. Not like this. "You're fucking gorgeous, you know that?"

Hunter's cheeks went pinker and Zach trailed his fingers over the hot skin in wonder. The man had fans mooning over him all the time and whole websites paying homage to his ass. But he still blushed.

"Shut up," Hunter muttered, then leaned in for a kiss that prevented any more compliments.

Zach wanted more. More kissing. More warm skin and molten hazel eyes. More Hunter.

He was achingly aware of his erection under Hunter's thigh, and of Hunter's poking him in the ribs. He would address those.

But first he wanted this.

He moaned in protest when Hunter eased back, the sound cutting off when a lube-slicked hand curled around his shaft. Hunter pumped him twice with a strong grip but Zach was already primed.

Shifting, Hunter spread his knees on the hard floor and positioned Zach's cock until it notched up against his entrance. The tightly furled muscles resisted as Hunter slowly lowered himself, his face screwed up in concentration. He should have looked ridiculous, but Zach's heart squeezed in his chest. He stared at Hunter in awe and held on for dear life, his fingers denting the soft skin over Hunter's hips to help steady him.

They both gasped when Hunter's muscles gave, and the head of Zach's cock slid inside.

Fucking hell, Hunter was *tight*. Zach gritted his teeth and watched Hunter's face, mesmerized by the little twitches and flutters of his eyelids as he relentlessly took Zach in. He didn't stop, not even a single pause, let alone a few short thrusts to allow himself time to adjust. He just...sat.

Zach shuddered as Hunter's ass came to rest in his lap. "*Fuck.*"

"Yeah," Hunter replied, sounding almost dreamy, his hips rolling in a slow, languorous circle that very nearly blew the top of Zach's head clean off. No one had ever looked as satisfied as Hunter did right then.

Hunter kept up the slow, filthy grind, pleasing himself and driving Zach half out of his mind in the process. Zach ground back as best he could while pinned to the floor by Hunter's weight—Jesus Christ, Hunter was *built*.

Hunter's hot gaze met his and he lifted himself up, dragging the length of Zach's cock through his tight hole, then dropping back down again with no attempt to slow the pull of gravity.

Their bodies met with a solid thump that seemed to energize Hunter, his thighs bulging as he lifted himself up again. Zach dragged Hunter as close as he could, capturing his mouth in a biting kiss. They both groaned while Hunter never stopped moving. He clung to the sink and a goddamn towel bar while Zach cupped his ass, doing what little he could to help while Hunter used his powerful body to do all the work.

Zach wished he could see them, wished he could witness what Hunter must look like from every angle. He said as much in a series of barely coherent gasps between kisses. He wasn't sure he was making any sense, but Hunter's groan suggested he managed to get the idea across.

The tight, hot clamp of Hunter's body around his cock was perfect, dragging Zach to the edge. He fought his orgasm and let more words fall out of his mouth, no longer caring if he was making sense. If he was saying too much. If he was embarrassing himself.

"You're so strong," he gasped between kisses. "So beautiful."

Hunter didn't seem to mind the compliments. Not anymore. So Zach let a litany of praise slip from his lips as Hunter sped up. His strength and control were still incredible, lifting until the head of Zach's cock barely remained lodged inside his body, then dropping into Zach's lap, launching a lightning bolt up Zach's spine every goddamn time.

It felt like Hunter could keep going forever, and Zach couldn't imagine a better torture. He told Hunter that, too. And that he'd dreamed of doing this again.

And that he'd missed Hunter. So much.

Hunter came with a sweet, inarticulate cry. He writhed in Zach's lap and Zach held on tight, the clench of Hunter's ass launching Zach into his orgasm. They clung to each other, their faces pressed together, their hands gripping too tight as they shook and gasped and shuddered.

When the storm passed, they collapsed in a heap against the wall, Hunter sprawled across Zach, his head on Zach's shoulder.

Zach kissed Hunter's forehead and stroked his hands through silky blond hair.

Hunter sighed with a gratifying amount of contentment.

"Welcome to Pittsburgh."

HUNTER STRETCHED out on the couch, beyond relaxed and in some zone where his muscles were jelly and his brain was up for little more than being happy and wallowing in it.

He thought this must be what it would feel like to win the Stanley Cup. Only soberer.

Not for the first time, he congratulated himself for buying the super-deep couch that had fairly screamed to be taken home and lounged all over. He'd been raised in a house full of sofas that his grandmother could sit on with a ramrod straight back and have her rigid spine delicately supported by the unyielding pillows. This couch, on the other hand, sucked you in and practically ate you.

"I love this fucking couch," Zach said, voice muffled against Hunter's chest. His long body was draped half on top of and all along the side of Hunter's.

Hunter smiled contentedly. "Yeah. The Beast is the best."

Zach snorted and murmured something like, "You named your couch."

It pleased Hunter that Zach seemed to be equally stupefied, barely able to articulate words as they became one with the furniture. After peeling themselves off the bathroom floor, they'd staggered up to Hunter's bedroom and showered. Hunter had been pretty fucking wrung out from practice followed by a mind-bending orgasm, but he'd still gotten hard when Zach gently washed him from head to toe. By the time Hunter was rinsed off, Zach had three fingers in Hunter's ass and was shouting his name as Hunter jerked them both to completion.

After that, Hunter had taken Zach on a tour of the house and even offered him a guest room, not wanting to assume. Zach had rolled his eyes and told him to shut up.

They'd ended up playing some pool in the newly finished game room, and Hunter had laughed at Zach's apparent relief at discovering what he'd called "a bachelor pad hidden in the basement." Hunter reassured him further by booting up the home theater. They'd made it halfway into Captain America before Hunter had Zach splayed out in a recliner, begging for relief while Hunter sucked him into next week.

Basically, it had been a perfect day so far, and he had hopes there'd be a few more highlight-reel moments before it was over.

This one right now, though, might be the best.

Hunter startled when his cat leaped onto his stomach. She paused to blink curious blue eyes at Zach.

Zach moved his hand slowly, letting her decide if she would tolerate his attention. "Come here, girl. I promise I won't bite."

She didn't look like she believed him, but not two minutes later, she was limp, her little body wedged between theirs while Zach's long fingers stroked her from ears to tail, over and over.

"She's very sweet," Zach observed.

"She's a slut," Hunter said affectionately.

Zach chuckled and stroked her again. The faint rumble of her low purr barely reached Hunter's ears.

Same, girl. Same.

"Her name is Gabby, right?" Zach asked.

Hunter smiled, secretly delighted by Zach's—probably unintentional—admission that he'd been reading Hunter's press. "Actually, no. I call her Gathy. People always get it wrong and I don't bother to correct them."

Zach lifted his head and propped his chin on a hand on Hunter's chest while still spoiling the cat with the other.

"Did you say *Gathy*?"

"Yup," Hunter said, adding a pop to the p.

A huge smile grew on Zach's face. "Oh my god. You named your cat *Gatherer*. Hunter and Gatherer." He buried his face against Hunter's chest and dissolved into his rare but adorable hiccup laugh that was *almost* a giggle and made Hunter feel like the king of the fucking world.

Hunter grinned and smoothed some of Zach's wild curls back from his face. They were longer than they'd been at Christmas, and Zach would probably say he needed a haircut—though Hunter would never agree.

Zach hummed and let himself be petted for a while. When he picked his head up again, his eyes roved around the room.

"Your house is really nice," Zach said.

"Yeah? Thanks. I know it's kind of..."

"Unexpected?"

Hunter let out a huff of laughter. "That's nicer than a lot of people are about it."

"People are mean about your house?" Zach asked, appalled.

Hunter shrugged. "No, not really. They like to tease me, though. Call me Suzy Homemaker and shit like that."

"Ha!" Zach said. "That's because most hockey players are assholes who live like inebriated fraternity brothers until they get married and then their poor, long-suffering wives have to try to mend their slovenly ways."

Hunter laughed, because Zach was absolutely correct. "Based on what I've seen, the wives often do that with the help of a housekeeper and an interior designer—not that I blame them."

"No designer for you?" Zach asked.

Hunter smiled smugly. "Nope." Then, less confidently, he admitted, "I like doing it all myself. The decorating."

"I'm impressed." Zach sweetened the compliment with a quick kiss. "It's beautiful."

Hunter glowed under so much praise. "Thanks."

"It's really…"

Hunter squirmed while he waited for Zach to finish his thought. It shouldn't matter what he said, but it *did.*

"…warm. Like, it's attractive and all that, but still comfortable and a place you can live, not a showpiece."

It was what Hunter had wanted. He'd been to a few teammates' houses where the kids were kept to their corner, and the rest was ready for a magazine shoot at a moment's notice. He shuddered just thinking about living in that kind of mausoleum.

"I wanted it for this," he admitted, gesturing around them.

Zach cocked his head. "What do you mean?"

"When you told me you were coming," Hunter began, worried he was going to reveal too much, but admitting it anyway, "all I could picture was this."

"Us crashed out on the couch?"

"Yes. With a bad game on the TV." He rolled his eyes at the team flailing around on the ice. "Take-out containers all over the coffee table and you half on top of me."

"What does that have to do with your decorating?" Zach asked, seeming genuinely curious.

"When I overhauled this house, this was what I was hoping for. I bought The Beast and installed the new mantlepiece and painted the walls cranberry red because then I'd have a place where I could be myself, and be *with* someone, and have it be this…"

"Comfortable?"

Hunter shrugged. "I was going to say *perfect*." He was afraid to meet Zach's eyes. Afraid he was going to scare him away.

Why did he always end up feeling so exposed? And what was it about Zach that made him willing to be vulnerable like this?

Zach rubbed a thumb over Hunter's cheekbone, nudging Hunter to look at him. Hunter glanced up, then met his gaze steadily when all he found was affection.

"You're not at all what I expected," Zach said, his thumb tracing Hunter's cheekbone again.

"What do you mean? You've known me since we were kids. I'm not that different, am I?"

Zach hummed. "I think we weren't fully formed back then. You're still the same person, but also more. You've grown, but not at all the way I imagined based on the way the press and your team's PR represent you."

"You look at all that stuff?" Hunter asked.

"Yeah. To be honest, I never stopped. I wanted to hate you, but I couldn't bring myself to lose track of your career. Even when I thought you were an asshole, I was proud of what you were doing."

Hunter's eyes burned. "Oh. That's—I don't know what to say." He ran his fingers through Zach's curls again. "Thank you."

Zach kissed him, sweet and lingering, before he settled with his chin propped on Hunter's chest again. "I guess I was surprised because your image is always so happy-go-lucky. The guy who has it all. Including"—Zach arched an eyebrow—"a gorgeous woman on his arm."

Hunter's smile was wry. "You should probably feel sorry for those women."

"Really?" Zach asked dubiously.

"They thought they were dating that happy-go-lucky guy who had it all, but instead they got me. A boyfriend who couldn't commit and had to close his eyes to get off."

Zach looked so sad it made Hunter's eyes burn again.

"Jesus, Hunter. I'm sorry."

"Eh, it was my own fault. I was convinced I could make myself bisexual."

"How'd that work out?" Zach asked with a wry smirk.

"Didn't take. Not even a little."

"What did the girlfriends think of the house?"

"Actually, I bought it about the same time I gave up dating. Sold my condo in a high-rise further downtown, stopped dating women, came out to Callum, and started admitting I like home decorating. It's been a big year," he said with a self-deprecating laugh.

In hindsight, it felt a little ridiculous.

Zach, though, didn't laugh. He just kept rubbing his thumb over Hunter's cheekbone.

"Hockey makes it difficult," Zach observed.

The words struck Hunter hard.

He hadn't realized how much it would mean to him that Zach knew and understood. To not have to explain. "It does. But sometimes I made it harder on myself than it had to be. Callum helped me see that."

"He seems like a good guy."

"He's more than just spank-bank material, that's for sure."

Zach grinned. "You're just jealous."

"Nah. I hear you replaced his poster, and if you need more material, you can lend me your phone later," Hunter said with a wink.

"Oh, *really*? Isn't there a rule against dick pics? What would your PR people say about this?"

"If you can't see my face, no one will ever know." Hunter grinned. "And I trust you. This would be strictly one-man spank-bank content."

"Strictly one man, huh?"

"Yup," Hunter agreed, his heart jumping in his chest. "I'm a strictly one-man kind of guy."

A smile stretched across Zach's face. "Well, then, I'll keep that in mind."

"You do that," Hunter said and pulled Zach into a kiss.

11

Mark drove Zach to the arena the next night since Zach had zero interest in attempting to get the hang of driving in Pittsburgh in Hunter's swanky ride. It felt decadent, particularly after his amazing but nerve-racking day on campus. CMU wanted him and they weren't being coy about it. Zach was flattered but couldn't completely shake the low-grade anxiety that he couldn't trust his own desires.

The program was great, though, and it had classes and tracks the other programs didn't. Zach watched the city of Pittsburgh slide past the window and reminded himself that he didn't have to decide anything on this trip.

Mark delivered him to a quiet side entrance where Zach gave his name and was promptly whisked below the arena. He was deposited into a beautifully appointed lounge full of gorgeous women and, in some cases, their offspring.

Being thrust into a room full of people who all seemed to know each other was the exact kind of social situation that made Zach go quiet, but those gorgeous women took pity on him and introduced themselves. It only took a couple of last names before he realized Hunter had arranged for him to be in the fucking family lounge.

He wished Hunter had given him *some* clue of how he was supposed to explain his presence there when asked. He ended up stammering out something about being an old friend of Hunter's and was relieved when everyone accepted it without a lot of questions.

A few minutes before puck drop, they moved as a herd into an enormous elevator that ferried them up to one of the suite levels. There, they settled into an absurdly luxurious space with an amazing view of the ice.

Zach felt spoiled but still had a pang of envy for the people sitting lower in the bowl with their popcorn and cheap beer in hand. He'd expected to be out in the crowd, just another anonymous fan, but he couldn't complain about the wide, padded seat and ice-cold Iron City lager.

Also, the wives and girlfriends were a fucking riot.

By the end of the first intermission, Zach knew more about the team's sex lives than they'd probably like him to, as well as some specifics about certain players' anatomy that might usurp his dreadful habit of staring at Hunter's poster when he jerked off.

Okay, that last part was a lie.

The game was a good one. Hunter was on fire from his very first shift. He could be a mouthy pain in the ass on the ice, and had been booed in more than one city, but the hometown crowd ate it up and could see he had wings on his feet tonight.

He scored a minute into the second period and everyone leaped to their feet, the women around Zach pounding on his back and high-fiving him like he had a damn thing to do with it. Hunter hugged his linemates in celebration, then turned to point at Zach before returning to the bench.

Zach's face was probably the same color as the ketchup on the cheap hot dog an attendant had been kind enough to get for him. The enthusiastic cheers in the suite turned to knowing grins and shoulder nudges from his new friends.

Zach tried to act like it wasn't a big deal.

But it was a huge fucking deal.

It also made him wonder if Hunter realized how much attention he was drawing to them.

Setting that aside until he could talk to Hunter about it later, Zach focused on enjoying the rest of the game. It wasn't hard. Hunter scored again—this time without turning seventeen thousand pairs of eyes in Zach's direction—and the good guys won.

As soon as the game ended, they all went back to the elevator and down to the family lounge. He assumed Hunter would come get him when he was done with his post-game routine. The TV in the lounge was tuned to the local coverage of the game and Zach smiled when Hunter came up on the screen. His face was still shiny and flushed except for a white slash across his forehead where his helmet had pressed against his skin. He'd long had the terrible habit of trying to dry his sweaty helmet-hair by scrubbing his hands through it, so it always ended up standing on end and at strange angles for these interviews.

It wasn't a wonder why the city of Pittsburgh adored him. He was fucking adorable.

Zach listened with half an ear, since the questions were always the same and the answers even more uniform and inane, until Hunter was asked who he had pointed to after his first goal.

Hunter's smile was alarmingly wide and warm. "Oh, yeah. I have a good friend visiting from back home." It was the truth, and it sounded so simple and innocent that the reporter didn't follow up.

Zach let out the breath he'd been holding and acknowledged maybe Hunter *did* know what he was doing.

Maybe.

Because Hunter was delayed by the interview, Zach was still waiting as more and more of Hunter's teammates arrived to collect their families. He tried not to be hideously shy as the wives and girlfriends he'd befriended introduced him to the players. He did all right until it was time to shake the captain's hand. He couldn't make words, his mouth opening and closing but no sound coming out. His face was so hot it was a wonder he didn't spontaneously combust.

He did eventually manage to stammer out a greeting and then

couldn't stop smiling once the captain and his girlfriend left the room.

The remaining wives and girlfriends were still teasing him about that when Hunter burst into the room.

"Zach!"

He rushed forward and hugged Zach before Zach could worry about what he should or shouldn't do. Zach managed a quick squeeze before Hunter stepped back.

Completely oblivious to the way his teammates were watching them, his gaze dropped and caught on Zach's chest, smile fading and eyes going heavy-lidded.

"Are you..." Hunter swallowed. "Are you wearing my jersey?"

"Of course." Zach tried to act casual. The truth was he'd bought the jersey and had it express shipped after Barnaby had promised he wouldn't regret it. When Zach had seemed dubious, Travis had laughed and assured him Barnaby knew what he was talking about.

He would apologize for doubting them. The way Hunter's eyes heated and trailed over him was going to be seared in his memory forever. Zach tried not to fidget and was intensely grateful the shirt was so long and baggy.

He was considering giving Hunter a kick in the shins to make him knock it off when two more players came through the door and made a beeline for them.

"Hunter! You ready to go, man?"

Juri Korhonen and Raf Zwyssig arrived with big smiles on their faces, their gazes moving between Zach and Hunter. Zach couldn't help feeling like the entire night was getting surreal. An entire NHL team was acting like it was no big fucking deal that Zach Bloom, lit-nerd from Moncton, New Brunswick, was hanging out with them.

These two were Hunter's closest friends on the team, and he'd been hearing stories about them for weeks, but somehow Zach had never quite connected in his brain that they were the same ridiculously hot, amazing hockey players he watched on TV all the time.

"Guys!" Hunter said, his expression almost...proud? "This is Zach."

Juri and Raf shook his hand enthusiastically.

"It's great to meet you," Raf said.

Juri echoed the sentiment and added, "It's good to have a face to put with the boy who makes Hunter smile at his phone all the time."

Zach's cheeks went hotter than they'd already been, while Hunter threw back his head and laughed. He punched Juri on the shoulder. "Don't embarrass me, you asshole."

He clearly didn't mind in the slightest.

Zach laughed, but his mind was reeling. It felt like the floor had shifted under his feet.

His legs felt wooden as he followed them out into the hall. The tunnels were quiet, and other than Raf and Juri ahead of them, no one was around, but Zach still jumped when Hunter slid his hand into Zach's.

Hunter immediately tried to pull away, his smile faltering, but Zach grabbed hold.

"We don't have to if you're not okay with it," Hunter said quietly.

Zach hated that he'd made Hunter look so unsure. "I'm just...I'm not sure what's okay and what's not."

"I didn't mean to put you on the spot." Hunter tried again to tug his hand free. "I'm sorry. I didn't think. I got excited and—"

Zach ran his thumb over Hunter's knuckles. "No, that's not it. I'm fine. But I'm worried."

Hunter watched him curiously, apparently unable to see the elephant in the room as it practically ran them down.

How did he not get it? "I'm worried about *you*," Zach explained.

Hunter looked confused. "Why?"

"I thought people couldn't know. The whole NHL thing." Zach waved his hand at the arena around them.

Hunter clenched Zach's hand tighter. "I haven't told Raf or Juri anything specific, but I haven't hidden anything either. I don't want to lie to my friends."

"Okay, I get that. They seem like great guys. But I'm not sure you're hiding much from the rest of the team either."

Hunter shrugged, but he looked determined. "I'm not going to make a big announcement, but I'm okay with it if they figure out I'm gay."

"Not that you should have to accommodate assholes, but will they be cool with it?"

"Not all of them, probably," Hunter admitted. "But they won't say anything."

"Are you sure? Seems like a big gamble if you're not ready to deal with what happens if they do."

Hunter sighed. "I know. But I really don't think that's what's going to happen. I'm not the only one, okay?"

"Really?"

When Hunter shot Zach a wry look, Zach rolled his eyes. "I mean, I know you're not the only gay man in the league. Or bi. Or whatever. I just didn't realize people *knew*. I figured they were as closeted as..."

"Me?"

"I was going to say Callum, actually. I've read a bunch of articles where he says he never dared to tell a soul."

"I'm sure there are plenty of guys like that, too," Hunter said, sounding sympathetic but also sad. "But there are also guys who just don't talk about it, publicly, but it's an open secret among their friends and teammates. I'm sure I don't even know half the total number for the exact reason that guys don't talk when they get traded. And if anyone in the press figures it out, they don't say anything because no one will confirm it and even they know it's an absolute shit move to out someone. And heck, a bunch of them are in the same boat."

Zach nodded, absorbing that as they walked around the lower tunnel. It made sense, but it was still hard not to be nervous for Hunter, even if he had proven, time and again, that he knew what he was doing when it came to managing the media.

Hunter sighed. "Look, maybe this is kind of shitty, but I don't want to be The Guy, you know? I don't want the asterisk next to my name forever. I don't want every mention of my game and my career to include *the first* and, for however long, *the only*. But that doesn't mean I can't tell people. And I hope that doesn't mean I can't have..."

"What?"

"You," Hunter said quietly, his voice hoarse.

Zach couldn't look away from Hunter's gaze. It was a wonder they didn't walk right into a pillar.

"Hey, you two! You coming or what?" Raf called from the door to the garage.

Zach smiled at Hunter, then picked up the pace, achingly conscious of Hunter's hand in his as they jogged to catch up with Hunter's friends.

HUNTER SPENT the car ride to the bar thinking about that smile.

Was that a yes?

To be fair, Hunter hadn't actually asked a question. He'd told himself they would have these four days together, and once they were over, he would do some serious thinking about what he wanted next.

But he already knew.

What he didn't know was what Zach wanted—and Hunter wasn't foolish enough to ask when they were minutes away from walking into a crowded bar full of teammates and at least a few fans. He could count on his teammates and even the mainstream press to keep his private life private, but he couldn't risk handing some fan all the material they needed to make their debut in amateur journalism on Deadspin.

Juri and Raf already had a table when Hunter and Zach came through the door. Hunter was relieved the place wasn't packed and they'd scored a booth tucked into the back corner of the bar area.

Hunter smiled gratefully at his friends as he slid into the banquette after Zach.

He was less grateful when Raf barely waited for Zach's ass to hit the seat before saying, "Zach! Tell us all about you."

Hunter narrowed his gaze on his delighted friends, hoping they'd take his warning.

They completely ignored him.

Fortunately, Hunter had a policy against being friends with

complete assholes, so he didn't worry too much as they peppered Zach with questions. Hunter listened with one ear while ordering them drinks and some food, hoping Zach didn't think he was overstepping by choosing for him.

He figured he was safe when Zach's knee pressed against his under the table.

While Zach started out a little haltingly, he got more comfortable as time passed, leaning back against the booth and laughing at Hunter when his friends inevitably started razzing him for something.

Back in high school, it had taken Hunter a while to understand what "shy" meant in someone like Zach. He'd always assumed the reserved shell was something fixed. That once you got to know him better, there would still always be a reticence, but that wasn't the case at all. Hunter could still remember how bowled over he'd been to learn that behind the quiet exterior, Zach was warm and snarky, and had a dry sense of humor Hunter adored. With people Zach knew and felt comfortable with, at least, he was as gregarious and goofy as anyone.

Hunter wanted to kiss his friends when they got Zach to that point in under fifteen minutes. When Zach leaned onto the table to argue the goalie's point of view about something, Hunter's eyes traced over his own last name stretched across Zach's back.

Fuck. He got a little hard every time he saw it.

He wondered how short he could cut this night without being rude or obvious about his need to take every single stitch of clothing off Zach *except* that fucking jersey.

He tuned back into the conversation when Zach mentioned his plans for grad school.

"I'm almost done with undergrad, then I want to go straight into a PhD program," Zach explained.

"That's cool, man," Raf said.

Juri nodded. "What do you study?"

"Right now I'm getting a degree in literature. But I'm also interested in history and sociology."

Hunter knocked their knees together. "That's why he's here this week. He's talking to Carnegie Mellon."

Raf and Juri looked impressed, and Hunter felt pride mix in with all the other emotions swirling in his chest.

"That's a really good school, right?" Raf asked.

Zach's cheeks went adorably pink.

Honest to fucking god, he was trying to kill Hunter.

"Uh, yeah. I guess. Mostly what I care about is that they've got this amazing program that's kind of perfect for me."

A zing of hope shot through Hunter.

Raf sent Hunter a look, like he knew just what was happening in Hunter's head, before turning back to Zach. "Yeah? What would you be studying, exactly?"

"The program is a PhD in Literary and Cultural Studies, but I can also do coursework in rhetoric and creative writing."

There was a long pause.

Hunter let out a disbelieving laugh. "Holy shit, I don't even know what that *means*."

Zach shrugged self-consciously and Hunter bumped his shoulder encouragingly while Raf and Juri asked him to try to explain what the hell that meant in terms a hockey player could understand.

Which Zach did, patiently and without being condescending, because he was Zach and he was kind of fucking awesome.

God, Hunter had it bad.

"Well, I hope you get in," Raf said.

"Oh, ah, I already did. They've accepted me."

Hunter froze, his eyes on Zach. "They did?"

Zach looked a little guilty. "I mean...I'm not sure what I'm going to do yet. I got into NYU, too, and I'm waiting to hear from Boston, so..."

Hunter leaned back and told himself to chill the fuck out. Zach had a lot to figure out and Hunter had promised himself he wasn't going to try to pressure Zach about CMU. That he'd already gotten into the program, the one he'd described as perfect, was the important part and Hunter would—*silently*—cling to that.

"That's great," Hunter said earnestly. "I'm sure Boston will come through, too. They'd be idiots not to want you."

"Thanks." Zach studied Hunter's face before looking back down at his beer. "I have a lot I have to consider."

"I'm sure," Hunter said, trying to sound supportive. Because he *was*, even if he wanted to grab Zach and shake him and beg him to come to Pittsburgh.

But that wouldn't be right. Hell, Hunter didn't know if Zach wanted anything beyond this week. Maybe Pittsburgh looked like a shit choice because Zach would have to deal with Hunter and tell him to leave him the fuck alone.

Raf, bless his fucking heart, saved Hunter from his mental spiral by asking Zach to explain what the fuck rhetoric was again. Hunter and Juri laughed. Zach absolutely lit up as he explained, his hands dancing through the air.

The conversation flowed for another twenty minutes before Juri stretched and announced he was beat and needed to head home.

Hunter popped up from the booth like it had burst into flames under his ass. He thanked his friends for hanging out and Raf for insisting he'd pick up the tab. Zach slid out after him, saying he hoped he saw Raf and Juri again soon.

Hunter took that as another good sign.

Raf and Juri agreed heartily and wished Zach good luck with school.

The blast of cold air when Zach and Hunter stepped from the crowded bar was a shock, particularly since they'd left their coats in the car. Zach shivered and sped down the sidewalk, his hands jammed in his pockets. Hunter would have kept up, but the view of his name stretched across Zach's broad shoulders and his number above Zach's tight, round ass was too good to pass up.

As soon as they got in the car, Zach slid his hand onto Hunter's thigh. "You good to drive?"

"Yeah, I only had the one beer. I'm good."

Zach's hand rubbed a little. "I'm sorry I didn't offer."

"I wasn't going to drink much anyway," Hunter admitted as he started the car and pulled into traffic.

"No? Is that an after-game thing?"

"Hell, no," Hunter said with a laugh, his foot heavy on the accelerator. "That's a *you look so fucking hot in my jersey I've had an erection for an hour* thing. An *I need all the self-control I can get* thing."

Zach's grin was a flash of white in the dim car. "Yeah?" He slid his fingers up Hunter's inseam.

Hunter clapped his hand over Zach's and held it still so he didn't end up driving into oncoming traffic.

Zach's hand wiggled under his but didn't try to escape his grip. "So, you like it? I wasn't sure…"

Hunter swallowed. "I like it," he croaked.

Zach leaned a little closer, his voice a rough whisper.

"*Good.*"

12

The truth was, Hunter was a simple man and Zach absolutely had his fucking number.

They barely made it through the door before clothes were flying in every direction. Having sex on the cold slate floor in the kitchen was not on the trainer's list of approved activities after a grueling hockey game, but Hunter couldn't care less when he was gripping the counter above him, his shirt half off, his face and chest pressed to the cabinet door and his ass sticking out for Zach to do with as he pleased. Hunter's knees, spread wide on the freezing stone, didn't ache. Absolutely nothing hurt—a first in his NHL career for the hours post-game—if he didn't count the slow burn of Zach sinking into him, stretching him open with a minimum of prep.

He begged Zach to go hard right from the start, his orgasm hovering like a fucking anvil above his head.

Zach curled around his back, pistoning his cock in and out of Hunter, and whispered, "This is what you get for wearing that fucking charcoal suit."

God, Hunter wasn't sure if he'd *ever* come that hard.

He wasn't surprised when Zach chose to wear a Michaelson jersey to the next game, too. That Zach stole the game-worn jersey from Hunter's own closet only made Hunter's problem worse. Zach told him he wanted to be able to smell the hint of Hunter's cologne through the entire game, and it just about undid all of Hunter's training and discipline. It was a miracle he scored. Hell, it was a miracle he could remember how hockey worked at all.

He begged off doing any post-game interviews, making a mental note to send Raf some fucking flowers or something when he volunteered to take Hunter's place.

Hunter showered and dressed in record time, aware of Raf and Juri smirking at him, but they didn't try to talk to him or slow him down as he flung his suit back on.

The charcoal one, because thank god for same-day dry cleaning, and two could play this game.

Zach waited for him in the tunnel outside the family lounge, and after a long, hot look that trailed over Hunter's body like a caress, he turned toward the parking garage without a word. It was some consolation to Hunter that he wasn't the only one suffering. Zach's cheeks had those tell-tale pink spots and Hunter seriously considered whether he could get away with blowing Zach in the back seat of his car, right there in the parking lot.

That was probably *not* how he wanted to come out to the team or management, though, so he slid behind the wheel and made straight for home.

Zach's hand wandered over the center console, but Hunter caught it before it could slither into his lap.

He had limits and he was pressed hard against them now.

It had been an amazing four days, and while Zach's departure in the morning was a weight lodged in Hunter's chest, the rush of arousal was a pretty good, if temporary, anecdote. It was hard to think about anything when his heart was pounding against his ribs and his spine tingled with the need to get Zach alone and naked.

The good news was Zach still seemed happy with what he'd learned about the program at CMU. The bad news was Hunter had no fucking idea what that meant. He was careful not to pry too much because he didn't want to add any pressure.

It was hard, though, when the last four days had shown him how good it could be.

He'd known he and Zach had a lot of catching up to do, but he hadn't expected to love hearing about Zach's travels so much. He hadn't expected Zach to sit with him on a FaceTime call with Hunter's parents and laugh about some of the dumb things they'd gotten up to way back when. He hadn't expected to want to dissect and debate his games and what the coaches had said in practice with Zach. And he definitely hadn't expected Zach to be into helping with any of that shit—even willing to watch tape with him as he prepped for the next game.

And it wasn't just about Zach being into hockey. It was just as good when Hunter had been on his iPad, trying to jam his brain full of whatever the coaches wanted him to see, while Zach had been tucked into the far end of the couch working on his school stuff, their feet tangled or in each other's laps, Gathy inevitably curled up on one of them.

None of it was anything Hunter had ever experienced before in a relationship, and now that he'd had a taste, he was more certain than ever about what he wanted. For the first time since he'd started in the NHL, he realized how fucking *alone* he'd been, and what it might feel like to not be.

He wanted that. And he was pretty fucking sure he knew who he wanted it with.

Oddly, it made him regret a lot of his past mistakes less. Zach had needed to go on those trips. He'd needed to kick ass at school and figure out what he wanted to do next. Hunter liked this version of Zach even better than the boy he'd loved years ago.

If Hunter had tried to stay with Zach all those years ago, he probably would have taken Zach's strength, humor, and affection for granted and not appreciated them for the incredible gift they were. Not figured out what he actually, truly wanted. What was possible.

And what he was willing to do to make that happen.

It was easy to believe anything was possible when Zach was clinging to his hand, his cheeks flushed as the two of them drove through the streets of Pittsburgh to get home and alone and into each other's arms.

Hunter had barely parked before they were flinging themselves out of the car and up the back stairs. Hunter had his coat off on the stoop, then he stepped into the mudroom and was faced with Zach's broad shoulders as he shrugged out of his parka.

MICHAELSON.

Jesus fuck, why was that so hot? It was his own name, for Christ's sake. It shouldn't be that thrilling.

But the surge of possessiveness, the burning desire to have his name on Zach and have people understand that what it really said was *MINE*, flowed hot through his veins.

Hunter couldn't look away as he tried to hang his coat on a hook, not caring when it slid to the floor.

It was a struggle not to keep stripping off clothes like they had last time, but it was their final night together, maybe for a long time—maybe forever—and Hunter wanted it to last.

Hunter threaded his fingers through Zach's and towed him into the house, past The Beast and the kitchen with its chilly, hard floor. Past the little bathroom in the hallway that Hunter was pretty sure he'd never be able to use again without becoming at least partially erect. When they reached the front hall, he towed Zach up the stairs, past the second floor with his office and the desk he would forever remember Zach bending him over—how he was ever going to be productive in there again, he didn't know—and the guestroom he'd offered Zach in a fit of delusion.

Finally, they reached the third floor and his bedroom. It stretched the length of the house, with the broad windows on the right overlooking the park, his bed on the left, and a sitting area around the fireplace on the far wall.

This was his haven, and Zach the only other person he wanted in here with him. He couldn't imagine that changing, either.

He closed the door, not bothering to turn on the lights, and drew Zach against his chest. Zach cupped his cheeks and pressed gentle kisses to his lips, their noses rubbing, his fingertips dancing over Hunter's ears and into his hair.

The erection Hunter had been sporting since he'd laid eyes on Zach after the game was still there, but that didn't feel as urgent, as painful or needful, as the ache in his chest.

He smiled up at Zach, barely able to see his face in the dim light, then crossed the room to the fireplace. He hit the switch and it came to life.

Zach spoke in a low voice from just behind him. "You know, as a Canadian, I feel honor bound to mock you for your faux fireplace."

"Just because it's gas doesn't mean it's not a real fireplace," Hunter said, not for the first time since Zach's arrival. "And you just don't want to admit having a fireplace in the bedroom is awesome."

Zach didn't disagree, humor sparkling in his eyes. Hunter watched, intrigued and delighted, as Zach pulled the duvet off the bed and spread it on the floor between the two reading chairs in front of the fireplace.

Hunter thought it should be too cheesy, too trite and cliché, but goddamn if his heart didn't skip a beat. When Zach's hand cupped his cheek again, Hunter leaned in like a flower turned toward the sun, an instinct so deeply rooted he couldn't possibly deny it.

Zach's kiss was sweet. And brief.

"I'll be right back." Zach yanked off his jersey and the shirt beneath as he moved away. He opened the nightstand drawer and dug around, his pale skin warmed by the firelight highlighting the shifting muscles in his back and shoulders.

Hunter wanted to kiss every freckle. Lick a path down the trench of his spine.

He was a professional athlete, goddamn it, *known* for his hand-eye coordination and strength under pressure, but his hands were shaking so hard he could barely get his shirt unbuttoned, never mind the absolute fumble he made of his tie. He managed to rid himself of both before Zach returned with condoms and lube. In the time it took Hunter to wrestle out of the rest of his clothes, Zach shucked his jeans and boxers and shoved the chairs aside so they had more space to stretch out on the floor.

Zach pulled Hunter down and rolled on top of him, propping himself up on his elbows. Hunter wrapped his legs around Zach's ribs and sighed when Zach's hips settled into the cradle of his thighs.

He thought maybe he'd like to spend the next thirty years doing pretty much this. Hockey was awesome, but *this,* this was the best.

Their kisses were long and slow. Hunter had felt like he was crawling out of his skin in the car, the intensity soaring as it had every other time they'd come together, but now the frantic need had been subsumed by a slow-burning fire that scorched him to his soul. Their bodies moved against each other, passion growing, but the kiss went on and on. When Hunter needed air, he dragged his lips across Zach's cheek while Zach nuzzled back, content to let Hunter kiss his eyelids, his chin, along his neck.

Zach's scent filled his head, and he buried his nose in the skin behind Zach's ear, trying to memorize everything about that moment to be able to savor it later.

Zach shifted to his knees to put a little space between them, and Hunter immediately missed the warmth of Zach's skin. The barely-there stroke of Zach's fingers over Hunter's cock and balls was sweet torture. He spread his legs, trying to give Zach all the room he could possibly want, and was rewarded when Zach trailed his touch down the seam of skin beneath Hunter's balls to his hole.

They'd had a lot of sex over the past four days, and Hunter was a little sore. Sore enough that he'd felt it during the game, which he knew wasn't the best idea. His body was his career and his job took a toll on it, so he did his best to protect himself when he wasn't on the ice.

That said, he had zero regrets, and he wasn't nearly so sore that he had any hesitation about letting Zach into his body again. Zach was always so careful with him. Even now, with Hunter opening for Zach's fingers so easily, he knew Zach wouldn't go too fast.

He whimpered when Zach's fingers left him, watching avidly as

Zach rolled on a condom. His hands weren't any steadier than Hunter's.

He reached for Zach. "Come here."

Zach tried to hold his weight off Hunter, but Hunter tugged until they were flush from hip to shoulder.

He curled his arms around Zach's neck, and they kissed. When Zach hooked an elbow under one of Hunter's knees and practically bent him in half, Hunter groaned. The stretch in his thigh after a long, hard-fought hockey game was its own pleasure, but it was nothing compared to the anticipation racing up Hunter's spine.

Hunter's breath hitched when Zach's cock bumped against Hunter's achingly sensitive hole.

"God, I'm going to feel this visit for a week and I can't think of anything better," he admitted with a half-laugh.

"Good," Zach growled, rocking his hips forward, his cock meeting resistance from muscles Hunter was honestly surprised had any left to give.

He let out a short breath, and the thick head slid inside him.

"Oh god," Hunter groaned, because the stretch was amazing, even when the sting edged into burn. He wondered deliriously if hockey had broken his brain when it came to processing pain.

He pressed his face to Zach's hot cheek. "How does this feel so good?"

"I don't know," Zach whispered, soothing Hunter with gentle kisses as he sank his cock deep in a single, devastating thrust.

Hunter's eyes fluttered shut, his entire existence honed down to Zach and the way their bodies moved together. They knew each other so well, better than four days could ever teach someone.

They were so much more than this visit. More than Christmas Eve. More than the year they had spent together when they were barely more than children.

Zach's hips worked in a steady, maddening rhythm, his knees shifting until he found the right angle and every thrust made Hunter cry out.

All Hunter could do was hold on. *Feel.*

Zach's face and shoulders shone in the flickering light, his cheeks flushed and hair damp. Hunter wondered if he'd ever sit and read by this fire again and not think of Zach. He hoped not.

He met Zach's eyes, the dark brown irises lost to blown pupils and the flickering shadows cast by the fire. His gaze, and the raw emotions Hunter didn't dare try to interpret, consumed and enveloped him. And that, in turn, made him feel bold.

Made him feel *certain*.

Zach's hands dug into Hunter's shoulders, his thrusts becoming more powerful, lighting Hunter up inside. The climb was swift and ecstatic, his orgasm slamming through him from one breath to the next, almost frightening in its intensity. His vision went dark, his cry hoarse and desperate.

Zach's hips lost their rhythm, each discombobulated thrust accompanied by a wounded sound from his throat. His grip on Hunter was almost painful, and Hunter clung back, sighing when Zach finally shuddered and cried out.

Zach collapsed onto the fluffy duvet beside Hunter, his heart pounding in his ears. He barely had the wherewithal to tie off the condom and put it aside before gathering Hunter into his arms and against his chest.

As always, Hunter curled into him. It made something in Zach unclench, something warm and sweet that was both scary and perfect. It should have been ridiculous to try to cradle a man built like Hunter. He was huge, muscled, incredibly powerful, and burrowing into Zach like he wanted to climb inside.

"I want to be with you." Hunter's voice was a scratchy whisper against Zach's heart.

For a moment, Zach wondered if he'd imagined the words. If he'd dreamed them up.

He ran a hand over Hunter's damp hair, then curled it around the back of his neck. "What?"

Hunter looked up at him and Zach was almost afraid to see

Hunter's face. Afraid to hear what he wanted to say. *Terrified* he wouldn't be able to give Hunter what he wanted and almost equally frightened that he shouldn't and would anyway.

"I want to be with you," Hunter repeated. "I want to make this work."

"But I live in Moncton," Zach said stupidly. It wasn't like Hunter didn't know that. And it wasn't what Zach was really worried about.

"I don't care," Hunter said. "Next year—"

Zach made a distressed noise he couldn't control. Before he could say anything, though, Hunter put up a hand.

"Hear me out. Please."

His head a mess of hope and dread, Zach nodded.

"I know you don't know where you'll be next year," Hunter said. "And I won't pretend I don't hope it's Pittsburgh, because you wouldn't believe me anyway."

Zach's chest got tight, the fear eclipsing the hope.

"But that's not what this is about. I want to be with *you*, Zachary Bloom. I want to be your partner and your friend. I want to travel with you and see the world through your eyes. To hear about your classes and help you avoid nervous barfing in front of your students and cheer for your beer league hockey team. That can be in Boston, or New York, or even back in Moncton."

Zach gaped at Hunter, overwhelmed by a rush of happiness. "Really?"

"Yes, really. *Of course.* I know the long-distance thing won't be easy, but I don't care. This is worth it. *You* are worth it. I'll spend my breaks wherever you end up and we'll have the entire off-season. I'll do whatever is needed in order to make this work."

Zach nodded, but his brain wouldn't stop chewing on the worries. "But it would be better if I came here," he said carefully.

"Sure, for the next year, anyway," Hunter agreed, then shrugged. "But after that, who knows? I'd like to think I'm going to be here for a long time, but we both know hockey is a fickle business, and if shit changes with my team, I could end up anywhere in the league. *Maybe*

I could try to end up on the same coast as you, but chances are I won't have any say in it."

Zach frowned. "As much as I'd like to have you near me, I wouldn't want you to choose a team for me. If you end up with options, you should choose the best team for you."

Hunter smiled. "Yeah, I get that, because I wouldn't want you to choose a school for me. I want you to go to the best school for you."

Oh. *Oh.* Zach released a shaky breath. Hunter *got it.*

Zach stroked his hand over Hunter's hair and smiled into those gorgeous hazel eyes. "Well then, in case it wasn't obvious, I want to be with you, too."

Hunter's entire face lit up. "Yeah?"

"*Yes.*" Zach laughed. He couldn't seem to stop touching Hunter. His hair. His cheeks. His lips. It felt so unreal to have this. To have *him*, again. "How did this happen? It seems too quick. Like we can't be this lucky."

Hunter chewed on his lip, then spoke softly. "I know how. At least for me."

Zach cocked his head, curious. "How?"

"I never got over you," Hunter said.

Zach's heart cracked open. He pressed their foreheads together and kissed Hunter sweetly. "Me either," he said, voice hoarse. It was shattering to finally admit the truth, to say what he'd hardly been able to believe. "God, me either. And I don't want to get over you this time, either."

"Okay," Hunter said as he burrowed into Zach and Zach held him tight. "Then we won't."

13

F our Months Later...
Hunter sat on the stoop outside the little brick apartment building, practically vibrating with excitement, and checked his watch again.

The campus-adjacent neighborhood was bustling with people, mostly students, even at the height of summer. It was young and hip and Hunter looked forward to spending time exploring the bright shops and sampling the countless restaurants.

But the best part about it, in his humble opinion, was that it was less than a mile from his house.

He'd walked over, taking the path through the park to make the distance even shorter. He liked that he'd have an excuse to pass the Phipps Conservatory on a regular basis. He and Zach had gone once this past spring when Zach had come to watch Hunter's playoff games and meet again with the faculty for his PhD program.

They'd been tucked in a quiet corner of the Orchid Room, fingers threaded together and bodies close, the first time Zach had said, "I'm still not over you."

Hunter had said it back. And they'd both kept saying it all summer long.

People might think they were weird, but they knew what it meant. They understood the vow hidden in those words.

Hunter's heart beat harder just thinking about it. He couldn't believe Zach was his and he was coming *here,* to the city that had adopted Hunter and made him feel like this could be his home. It hadn't been an easy decision for Zach, but Hunter had made certain Zach knew he had Hunter's support no matter what, and now he couldn't and wouldn't be sorry with how it had all shaken out.

Hunter felt more grounded, more sure about himself and what he was doing, than he ever had before. Hockey had always been the dream, and he'd been so damn sure that being drafted was the first step toward the exact life he'd always wanted.

It turned out he'd had to retrace his steps all the way back to Moncton to find that.

It also turned out that trying to live a life without regrets had made Hunter a better hockey player.

Go figure.

He'd absolutely kicked ass in the playoffs, and while they hadn't gone all the way, management had taken notice and decided Hunter was an important piece for the future of the franchise. Hunter's agent had negotiated a new and pretty fucking amazing contract over the summer, a year before Hunter's current one was up, and he wouldn't be going anywhere for three to five years, at least.

Plenty of time for Zach to finish his degree and then...

Well, they'd figure that out. Together.

"What are you smiling about?" Zach asked as he strolled up the sidewalk.

Hunter's smile got wider as he looked up at his beautiful boyfriend. "How sexy *Dr. Bloom* sounds."

Zach's cheeks went pink. "Shut up," he mumbled, looking down at his beat-up sneakers. He was grinning, though, clearly pleased.

Hunter climbed to his feet, running his hand down Zach's arm. They'd only been apart three days, but seeing Zack settled something in Hunter. "Where did you come from? I was expecting you to pull up front."

Zach had driven the U-Haul by himself down from Moncton, which Hunter hadn't loved. Unfortunately, Hunter had already committed to spending the last few days taking care of some obligations with a sponsor, but Zach and Hunter had still agreed this was the best time for Zach to make the move. Callum, Barnaby, and other friends had helped Zach move out of his old place before sending him off to Hunter.

"I found a spot by the back door. I wasn't sure if there'd be a space out here and parking that thing is a pain in the ass, so I took a spot I knew would work."

Hunter turned, ready to start unloading, when a huge, ostentatious SUV parked in the empty spot right in front of them.

Hunter rolled his eyes, waiting until the doors opened before calling out, "Do you two honestly not have a single car between you that I'm not embarrassed to be seen with?"

Raf laughed as he fell out of the passenger seat, while Juri shot Hunter the one-fingered salute from across the hood.

Zach eyed the car. "Is that a purple Bentley?"

Hunter snorted. "It is."

"Jesus," Zach muttered, "what will the neighbors think?"

Hunter cracked up. Juri and Raf looked curiously at him while they offered Zach hugs and backslaps. Two people came out of the building and Hunter stepped aside to give them room to come down the stairs.

When that didn't happen, he looked up and saw their faces. *Oops.*

"Safe to say the neighbors are already going to wonder about you," Hunter observed in a low voice, so he wouldn't be overheard. The two twenty-something-year-old men engaged in an epic bout of elbow nudging, as if the other might not notice who was standing on their stoop.

Zach pretended he didn't see them. "How was asking you guys to help me move in a good idea?"

"Because we're big, strong, manly men," Raf said.

He and Juri proceeded to strike a series of muscleman poses.

Zach's neighbors watched, agog.

Zach buried his face in his hands.

Hunter rolled his eyes and led the way up the stairs. "Okay, losers, let's get this done."

He smiled and thanked the neighbors when they stepped aside to make room for them. Neither one seemed capable of making actual speech.

Hunter had been hoping there wouldn't be any hockey fans in the building, but no such luck. He could only hope things got less awkward as time went on.

He understood why Zach wanted his own place in Pittsburgh. Hell, Hunter agreed. Zach needed to get established and settled into his new city on his own. That said, Hunter had every intention of being around here *a lot*, and it would be nice if the neighbors didn't make it weird.

He looked back at his friends, who appeared to be engaged in some kind of slap fight. Honest to fucking god, one would never know they were adults with real-life jobs and responsibilities.

Still, Hunter was grateful to have them in his life.

Even if they bitched and moaned. A *lot*.

In spite of that, they got Zach's apartment unloaded from the truck and mostly distributed into his new home in a couple of hours. Hunter ordered pizza to go with the beer he'd stocked in the fridge when he'd come by the night before, using the key already secured on his keyring.

He figured the least he could do was feed his friends after they lugged that fucking monster red plaid couch up two flights of stairs. He'd forgotten it had a pull-out bed, and he'd tried very hard not to laugh when Juri had started swearing in Finnish, and Raf had responded in German *and* French.

Though Hunter had stopped feeling nearly so charitable when the two of them wouldn't stop waggling their fucking eyebrows at him as they assembled the bed.

He almost regretted taking them out to dinner a couple of nights ago to tell them Zach was his boyfriend. Then again, the assholes had just sat there looking at him like they were still waiting for him to tell them something new versus something they'd figured out on their own months ago.

He'd made an inappropriate hand gesture and they'd ordered a stupidly expensive bottle of champagne and mocked him mercilessly for an hour.

It had been pretty perfect, honestly.

But not so perfect that Hunter wasn't happy to boot them out of Zach's apartment once they'd been fed and had sufficiently recovered from moving the furniture. He and Zach watched from the front window and laughed when they came out of the building and discovered a ticket on that stupid, overpriced, gas-guzzling blueberry of a car.

"I should pay that ticket," Zach said. "They were here to do me a favor."

"Nah. Think of it this way, you probably made the meter-person's day. If I had that job, I can't imagine a car I'd want to ticket more."

Zach chuckled. "True."

Hunter watched his friends drive off, then slid his arms around his boyfriend's waist and nuzzled the back of his neck.

"God, I missed you."

ZACH LEANED into Hunter's hold. He couldn't believe he was here. With Hunter. That somehow, after everything, it had worked out.

He hadn't realized he could be this happy. This *hopeful*.

"I missed you, too," he said, turning in Hunter's arms and catching his mouth in a soft kiss. "Thank you for helping me move in. And for lending me your friends."

"I'm pretty sure they're your friends, too, now."

Zach hoped so. He liked them a lot. And it was nice to know they would be on the road with Hunter this season while Zach was back in Pittsburgh.

Zach wasn't certain how everything would shake out, but he was pretty sure he'd be spending a lot of time at Hunter's house, even when Hunter was out of town.

In fact, he'd only signed a six-month lease, but he hadn't told Hunter that yet. He had the option of extending it another six months if he didn't think he was ready. If Hunter wasn't ready.

Though he'd spent most of the last three hours thinking about Hunter's beautiful home, and The Beast, and Gathy, and he'd had to constantly remind himself why moving into this place was necessary.

At least for now.

He and Hunter had spent almost every night together for the past couple of months, first here in Pittsburgh once Zach's semester was finished, then back in Moncton while Zach packed up and Hunter trained for the new season. They'd spent a lot of time with Barnaby and Travis, as well as Callum and Alexei and their extended family.

It would *always* be surreal to Zach that he now counted Callum Smythe-Morrison as a friend. And Alexei had gone so far as to offer to ride shotgun on the drive down here, but Zach had declined. Alexei had a wedding to prepare for—one which Zach and Hunter would head back up to Moncton for in late August.

Which reminded him...

"Hey, did you get the tickets for the wedding? What do I owe you?"

Zach was concerned by the cagey look on Hunter's face. For the most part, Hunter was good about the disparity in their finances. He understood that Zach never, ever wanted to be a freeloader.

When Zach narrowed his eyes, Hunter rushed to say, "I'll text you the ticket price when I'm at my computer, cool? You can Venmo me or whatever."

Zach smiled, relieved. "Great. Thanks."

"But, uh..." Hunter stopped and licked his lips and Zach's concern returned. "Remember how we were going to take the next three weeks to get settled in here and spend some time, just the two of us? Maybe take some day trips? But, you know, I said we shouldn't make any set plans?" He gave Zach his most winsome smile.

Hunter was babbling, which meant Zach had good reason to be nervous. "...Yes?"

"Well, one of my sponsors asked the team to send a bunch of us over for this event thingy for a couple of weeks and they said we could each bring one person with us and I asked them to be sure the guests weren't going to end up in some PR fluff piece and they said they'd be kept totally off camera so I gave them your name and said you'd be my plus-one or whatever and I figured that wouldn't be a big deal because Raf is bringing his brother and the sponsors are paying for, like, all of it so—"

Zach pressed his fingers over Hunter's mouth to stem the tide of verbal diarrhea.

Hunter blinked at him, those beautiful hazel eyes worried.

"You signed us up for a two-week trip *where*?" Zach asked, pulling his fingers away.

Hunter let out a breath. "Beijing."

Zach wondered if the summer heat had fried his brain. "Did you say *Beijing*?"

"Yes."

"In China?"

"That's the one."

Zach honestly didn't have any idea what the fuck to say.

Hunter towed him over to the couch and pushed him to sit, then knelt between his legs. "I'm hoping this is a good surprise," Hunter said. "I mean, that's what I wanted it to be and why I didn't tell you a month ago when they asked me. I really want to travel with you, see more of the world, and I know you like to travel between semesters and I'm at least partly the reason you weren't able to this summer."

"It *is* a surprise," Zach allowed. Then he focused on Hunter's worried face, and he smiled. "An amazing one."

Hunter smiled back. "Yeah?"

"Yeah. God, *Hunter*," Zach said, struggling to find the words to convey how amazing it truly was. He kissed the bejesus out of his ridiculous boyfriend. "We're going to China. Holy shit. Beijing is totally on my bucket list."

"I figured it might be," Hunter allowed.

Zach ran his fingers down Hunter's cheeks. "Thank you."

"You're very welcome. Though, in this case, I'm not actually doing much. I just wanted you with me. I want to travel with you and see new things and hear your thoughts and tell you mine, you know? I want to explore new places and eat food that freaks me out and then be surprised when I love it or laugh when I don't. I just...I—"

Zach put his fingers over Hunter's mouth again and said the words that had been in his heart for months, the ones he'd wanted to say that night in front of the fire in Hunter's bedroom, the ones that had been on the tip of his tongue a thousand times since.

"I love you."

Tears welled in Hunter's eyes and Zach felt as though someone had reached inside his chest and squeezed a fist around his heart.

"I love you, too," Hunter said, his voice hoarse. "So much."

"And I'm never going to get over you," Zach admitted.

Hunter pressed their foreheads together, his hands cupping Zach's cheeks.

"No," he agreed, kissing Zach sweetly. "Never."

ABOUT THE AUTHOR

Samantha Wayland has three great loves in life: her family, writing books, and hockey. She is often found apologizing to the first for how much time and attention is taken up by the latter two, but they forgive her because they are awesome and she clearly doesn't deserve them.

Sam lives with her family—of both the two- and four-legged variety—outside of Boston. She is a wicked passionate New Englander (born and raised) who has been known to wax rhapsodic about the Maine Coast, the mountains of New Hampshire and Vermont, and the sensible way in which her local brethren don't see a need for directional signals (blinkahs!).

Her favorite things include dirty martinis, tiny Chihuahuas with big attitude problems, and the Oxford comma.

Sam loves to hear from readers. Email her at samantha@samanthawayland.com, visit her website at www.samanthawayland.com, or find her on Facebook (Samantha Wayland), Twitter (@samwayland), or Instagram (SamWayRomance). If you want to learn more about what she's working on and hear about her writing process, be sure to join her reader group on Facebook, Sam's Wonderland.

Be sure to sign up for Sam's newsletter to hear about sales, new releases, works in progress, and to get access to bonus content. You can sign up via her website or by going here.

www.ingramcontent.com/pod-product-compliance
Lightning Source LLC
Chambersburg PA
CBHW051953170626
46808CB00007B/2598